The Best of
Pony Club Stories

The Best of

PONY CLUB

Stories

Purnell

SBN 361 04177 2
Copyright © 1978 Purnell and Sons Limited,
Published 1978 by Purnell Books, Berkshire House,
Queen Street, Maidenhead, Berkshire,
from stories first published in Pony Club Annual 1968, 1969, 1972, 1973, 1974, 1975, 1976, 1977
Made and printed in Great Britain by Purnell and Sons Limited,
Paulton (Bristol) and London

CONTENTS

No Pony Like Tango *by Patricia Jamieson*   7

A Matter of Background *by Primrose Cumming*   13

The Noble Cause *by Elizabeth Rigbey*   31

That Pony Will Have to Go *by Nicola Herd*   42

Jennifer's Pony *by Cdr. H. Falcon-Steward*   47

A Promise to Dawn *by Veronica Riches*   53

A Polo Conversation *by Pauline Gerrard*   60

Double Trouble *by Carol Vaughan*   68

Doctor's Orders *by Jennifer Wharton*   83

Chop and Change *by Josephine Pullein-Thompson*   89

Nicky Would Not Move *by Alicia Moore*   108

The Badger Brigade *by Selina Charlton*   114

INTRODUCTION

It was lovely to be given an excuse for re-reading all the stories published in the Pony Club Annual and, though this anthology couldn't include the entire collection, I hope the following pages will give equal pleasure to many others.

The hardest part in compiling the anthology was in trying to decide which of the many excellent stories written by regular contributors to the annual should be included and (even harder) which should be left out. My own favourites are not necessarily the same as those of our readers but, since I couldn't arrange an opinion poll, it had to be a personal choice.

So I have chosen stories that particularly appealed to me at the time they were published and which still seemed just as good when I re-read them. The regular contributors to the annual are represented by four thoroughly readable and entertaining stories —Josephine Pullein-Thompson's "Chop and Change", Carol Vaughan's "Double Trouble", Primrose Cummings's "A Matter of Background" and Elizabeth Rigbey's "The Noble Cause". I hope you will enjoy these (and all the others) as much as I have.

Genevieve Murphy

No Pony Like Tango

by PATRICIA JAMIESON

"I can remember it all now," I said to Dr Melloham. "I was approaching the last jump, a wall, four feet nine inches high and four feet one inch wide. Popcorn took off all right, but in mid-air he realised that he wasn't going to clear the jump, and he began to panic. He struggled to stretch out a bit further, but he didn't make it. I felt him lurch underneath me, and the next thing I knew we were plunging downwards towards the ground, which seemed to be rushing towards us. I heard a woman scream, and then, with a dull thud accompanied by a clatter of falling bricks, we landed.

For a moment all was quiet and still, and then I heard people shouting, and I saw a group of men running towards us. Popcorn had landed heavily on my back, and neither of us moved. I heard someone say to call for a vet. and a doctor. Someone else said that a vet. wasn't needed, because anyone could see that Popcorn had broken both of his front legs, and he would have to be put down.

"Tears began to run slowly down my face, when I realised that I would never see Popcorn again. Then about five or six men managed to lift Popcorn while another man pulled me out. By this time a doctor had arrived on the scene. He carried me to the First Aid tent, and then he examined me. After a few 'hums' and 'haas', he phoned for an ambulance. From that time onwards I was in agony. I couldn't feel my legs at all, and I had a very bad backache, which was not surprising considering the weight that they had taken. As I went out of the field in the ambulance, I began to cry helplessly, when I thought again of Popcorn being put down. That was the last that I saw of him." I stopped talking, and looked up at Dr Melloham. "Go on," he said quietly.

"There's not much more to say," I said. "I was taken to the hospital, had numerous operations, X-rays, and examinations, and was told that I would never walk without a limp again."

I looked down at my shrivelled, deformed legs, and hated the sight of them. Dr Melloham got up from his seat, and came over to me. "I suggest that you take up a sport to get your mind off your legs. Do you think that you could ride again? It would be very good for your legs."

I looked up at him and smiled. "I guess I could ride again. Anyway I'll have a jolly good try."

"That's the spirit, my girl," said the doctor. "I'll have to go now. Try to start riding as soon as possible. I'll see you again on Wednesday. Goodbye," Dr Melloham left the room, and I went down to my parents. I explained to them that I wanted to start riding again, and they were very pleased, because they had both been keen riders in their time.

That afternoon I went to the local riding-school to have my first lesson. The riding-mistress said that I had great possibilities in riding, and that I was the perfect owner for a pony that she knew was for sale, and was I interested? I said that I would have to ask my parents first, but I was pretty sure that they would say yes. The riding-instructress then said that if I wanted to try out the pony, he would be at the riding-school the next day, and I could ride him on my lesson.

That night I told my parents about the pony, and they were willing to buy him, providing he was all right, and he didn't cost too much. So the next day at 2.30 p.m., we arrived at the stables ready

We were plunging downwards towards the ground

to try out the pony. The riding-mistress was called Sue, and she had tacked the pony up ready for me. She told me that the pony, Guitar Tango, was not very quiet, but he was easy to handle. He stood about 13.2 hands, and he was a palomino in colour with a lovely, long mane and tail. He was six years old. I took Tango out of his box, and mounted by the mounting-block.

I then rode into the field, where I had my lesson with Sue. I walked, trotted, cantered, and jumped a jump. Much to the delight of my parents, I had not lost my nerve because of my fall, and I was quite willing to jump again. We discussed the price of Tango, and his possibilities as a jumper. In the end my parents bought him for £100. We agreed that Tango should be kept at the stables, and that I should go up every week-end and look after and ride him.

When I went back to school on Monday, I was telling my best friend Cathy about Tango when Alison Welch, a snob in my form, came up and overheard me telling Cathy.

Alison had an equally snobbish friend called Diana Mackey. They both owned thoroughbred ponies, and they were competing in the novice class at the Pony Club show. Diana came to join Alison by me, and the pair of them started bragging about how they would both win the novice class. I couldn't stand it any longer. I knew that they were doing it to spite me. In a loud voice I said that I also was going to enter for it on my 'famous show-jumper', who was bound to win. Alison and Diana gave short, mocking laughs and walked away. "What have you said?" asked Cathy. "Now Alison and Diana will expect you to win. If you don't then you'll never hear the end of it."

"I know," I said meekly. "I was a bit of a fool to say that, but they were doing it to annoy me. Anyway, I'm going to try to win, even if I don't."

Because of what I had said, I went up to the stables every Saturday and Sunday, and most days after school, when I didn't have much prep. Tango improved enormously, and after a few weeks he could jump three feet eleven inches with a three foot spread. I was surprised that my legs also had improved. There was

I then rode into the field

no time to think about them, so they didn't hurt or ache.

We arrived at the show-ground in good time, with an hour to spare, and I wasn't jumping until tenth. I entered, and then collected my number, which was 537. Then I limped back to the trailer, and unboxed Tango. I tacked him up and quietly rode him round the field. I caught a fleeting glimpse of Alison and Diana, galloping their ponies up and down, and forcing them over practice jumps that were too high for them. I only let Tango walk and trot and have one short canter, so as not to tire him.

It seemed too soon when I was called into the ring to jump. Alison and Diana had already been, and they had both jumped clear. I was very nervous when I rode into the ring, so I trotted Tango round once or twice to settle our nerves. Then the bell went.

I rode him at the first jump, which was a brush of about two foot. He popped over this easily, and went on to the next jump.

The next six jumps were all ranging from two foot six to three foot. Tango cleared them all easily, and we cantered through the finish. As I rode out of the ring I heard Alison say that my clear round was just a fluke, and I was bound to go hay-wire in the jump-off. Ignoring this remark I went over to Sue and my parents. Sue had come third in the open jumping. No one else went clear.

In the jump-off the height of the jumps was raised from three foot to four foot four inches. Alison was eliminated, and Diana got eighteen faults. I rode into the ring and used my stick to get him over the first three jumps. The course had been shortened to numbers one, two, three, five, seven, and eight. This shortened course entailed a few sharp turns, but Tango, in his usual clever way, managed them, and we rode out of the ring with a triumphant four faults, which we collected at number eight. We had won!

I flung my arms round Tango's neck, and told him what a clever pony he was. After I had collected my prize, I led Tango back to the trailer, where my parents and Sue were waiting. My mother said that I was hardly limping.

"Who cares about a silly little limp," I answered, "when they've got a super jumping pony like Tango?"

12

A Matter of Background

by PRIMROSE CUMMING

"The whole trouble is," said Veronica, "that our parents haven't a horsy background."

"How d'you mean?" asked Harriet, gaining time to consider her elder sister's statement.

"No tradition of horses," Veronica warmed to her subject. "They didn't have ponies as children, never learnt to ride. That's why we don't do as well as we might."

The girls were resting from their labours of committing a dressage test to memory. Harriet had the paper, which was damp from Marigold's interested nostrils. Their practice area was marked by sticks at the corners with convenient plants and cow-pats acting as markers. They also had two jumps made of bean poles and oil drums and one handsome slatted arrangement, salvaged when their father put up a new bench in the greenhouse. Marigold, glowing in the sun, nearly as orange as her namesake and almost as rotund, took advantage of the conversation to graze. Grey Smoky gazed intently at the view as if expecting hounds to burst into the summer landscape.

"Well, it is true," agreed Harriet. "What's made you suddenly

"Ordinary trot at B," she sang out as they walked by

think of it?"

"Overhearing Miss Bryant at the last rally when that Ellis boy came with the wild pony. She said his parents shouldn't have bought such an unsuitable pony, but then they had no horsy background."

"But Marigold and Smoky are all right, even if they're not exactly champions."

"I know. But we could do better with them if Mummy and Daddy understood more. Look when I wanted a Kimblewick. Daddy said, couldn't I hold Smoky in a snaffle? I said it wasn't to hold him, but to keep him balanced. But when he heard what a Kimblewick cost he said he wasn't going to give all that for another bit of ironmongery when I could manage Smoky all right with the snaffle. If he rode himself he would understand."

"You never thought of a Kimblewick until Ann Jones had one," said Harriet.

"That's the point. Her parents hunt. They knew."

"Well, there's not much we can do about our parents' background now," sighed Harriet. "It's only a week to the Event, so we'd better get on. My turn to see you through the Test."

Veronica and Smoky set off while Harriet glanced to and fro between them and the paper.

"Ordinary trot at B," she sang out as they walked by.

"Haven't got to B."

"You have; past it. It's that clump of moon daisies."

"'Tisn't. It's that thistle."

The Test was held up while they argued. Finally a pacing out proved Harriet to be right.

"It's so frustrating," complained Veronica. "Horsy parents would fix up a proper arena *and* decent jumps."

"It's not surprising people like Ann and Jerry Redman win everything," agreed Harriet. "Mr Redman buys and sells ponies, so of course he's got proper jumps and an arena and a cross-country course for Jerry to school them over."

"If only Daddy was a Master of Hounds or a horse dealer," said Veronica wistfully.

"Wouldn't it be super? Or if Mummy just had a riding school or bred palominos."

The lunch bell interrupted their pipe dreams. Removing the ponies' tack and leaving them to roll, they joined their mother. Mr Bell went to London daily.

"They've 'phoned to say the box will be here at eight-thirty on Saturday," Mrs Bell told them at lunch. "Then you go on to pick up Tony and Maureen."

"If we had a trailer, we needn't start so early," remarked Veronica.

"Our car won't pull a trailer, and poor Daddy couldn't drive up to the office in a Land-Rover."

"If Daddy was a farmer he wouldn't have to go to London," observed Harriet.

"Well, he isn't. You're lucky to live in the country and have ponies. How is the dressage going?"

"Dress-arge," Veronica corrected. "Pretty awful. We keep losing the arena."

"Well, it's the part round the countryside you really enjoy, isn't it. Nice and natural."

When the box called for them on Saturday, the ponies were ready tied up in the garage, tails bandaged and hoofs stickily oiled. Next time Mr Bell went to mow the lawn he would find the oil can empty. Red-faced Mr Pargeter, the driver, helped load.

"That Marigold, her shadow don't get no less," he observed.

Mrs Bell helped to hand up the gear.

"What a lot of luggage these ponies need, everything from buckets to beauty-cases. Here's a snack to keep you going and I'll meet you with the lunch. I'll be in time to walk round the course with you, that will give Porgy a nice run before it all starts."

Porgy was the pug.

They picked up Tony Robinson and his pony, Harlequin, and also Maureen Telford who had hacked Squib three miles to join him. Four of them in the cab with Mr Pargeter was a bit of a squash. Every time he changed gear Harriet, sitting next to him, had to

16

The ponies' tack was removed and they were left to roll

draw her right knee up to her chest.

"How many rosettes are we bringing back?" asked Mr Pargeter.

They giggled uncertainly. As Squib was a show-jumper Maureen seemed to have the best chance. Especially as, Harriet reflected, Mrs Telford had show-jumped a lot before she had Maureen. Tony's parents were both artists, and it was more than likely that when buying Harlequin they had been more influenced by his picturesque black, brown and white markings than by his jumping ability.

Arrived at the site of the One Day Event, they parked next to the box of Redman, the dealer. Jerry's pony was already unboxed and he was unwinding yellow leg bandages while Mr Redman put finishing touches to the plaits.

While Tony and Maureen went off to inspect the cross-country course, Veronica and Harriet filled in the time waiting for their mother with a bit more grooming. Their eyes strayed enviously to their neighbours. After a time Jerry looked in their direction and acknowledged them with a nod and a 'Hello!' Although rather small for his age and pale, he had an air of tough efficiency that never failed to impress the sisters. The row of new-season's rosettes decorating the cab of the Redman's box proved that this air was not just put on.

Mr Redman had a more genial manner.

"Your ponies look well," he remarked, "though you are getting quite big enough for the grey, Veronica. Topthorn, here, would carry you a treat, only I've already got a buyer if he does well today."

Jerry gave a sharp exclamation which made them stare. But he turned his back, so they studied Topthorn, the dark bay pony responsible for most of the new rosettes.

"He's super," said Veronica enviously.

Topthorn was a hard, keen type, tuned to a high pitch. His coat had the deep glow of an old oil painting, unmarred by a speck of scurf. You could have parted his tail and found the black hair clean and shining right down to the skin.

"Being able to turn a pony out properly must be inbred," she decided. "We can never hope to do it."

Mr Redman had a more genial manner

Maureen and Tony came rushing back.

"It's a stinker!" cried Tony. "I'll never get round."

"Squib may just do it, but it'll be touch and go."

"Is that the cross-country?" asked Mr Redman. "Time they upgraded it a bit. Standards have risen. It's been so easy in the past that the dressage marks counted for too much. Eh, Jerry?"

"S'pose so," responded Jerry.

Veronica and Harriet were much alarmed.

"Is it really stiff?"

"There's a great wide open ditch and a big stack of logs and a perfectly horrible sort of thing over a ditch into the wood."

"That would be the Trakener, something they haven't had here before," observed Mr Redman with satisfaction.

Just then Mrs Bell and Porgy arrived, and with troubled minds Veronica and Harriet set off to see the course for themselves.

Their spirits sank lower with each obstacle. The open ditch seemed like a gulf; a stack of firewood had to be jumped with the chopped ends on; a cattle-pen at the side of a barn demanded a difficult turn. They tried to draw comfort from the comments of other riders.

"What do they think this is? Badminton?"

But others supported Mr Redman's attitude.

"At last we've got something worth jumping."

Ann Jones, when they encountered her, had no sympathy for their fears.

"You'd jump things like this out hunting without looking at them."

"Bet I'd look, and so would Marigold," muttered Harriet.

"*We* don't hunt every week," added Veronica.

The Trakener was the last straw. A stout larch pole lashed between two trees parallel above a wide ditch: it was a barrier, not a jump.

"What do they call it?" Mrs Bell interrupted their groans.

"A Trakener, sort of German fence," said Veronica.

"How ridiculous, building a nasty foreign thing in English

countryside! I shouldn't take the ponies in if you think it's too much for them."

Mrs Bell's voice was a carrying one, and both Veronica and Harriet were aware of smiles from a family group with riders, labradors and shooting sticks nearby. The group had 'horsy background' written all over them.

"Of course we must go in now we've entered," said Harriet loudly.

"It's not that the ponies couldn't do it," added Veronica. "It's just that we've had nowhere where we could school them properly."

"Do we have to see any jumps in the wood?" asked Mrs Bell.

"No. It only goes through a little bit of the wood and the next jump is out again. I bet it's a beast."

"I'm glad we don't have to go in the wood," said Mrs Bell. "I'm always afraid of Porgy's eyes."

This brought more signs of amusement among the labrador party.

Knowing in their hearts that they would never get beyond the Trakener, if as far, it was ironical to find the remaining obstacles less frightening.

They returned to the box in a depressed state and unable to do justice to the nice picnic lunch their mother had provided. Alarmed by this, Mrs Bell returned to the idea of scratching their entries.

"It's meant to be a pleasure. Why risk injuring yourselves and the ponies doing something that frightens you?"

"We're not *frightened,*" Veronica and Harriet cried in unison, feeling sure the Redmans had overheard.

"The ponies want more schooling," repeated Veronica.

"A bit sticky, eh?" asked Mr Redman.

"They shouldn't be, all the grooming they've had," said Mrs Bell.

Redman grinned, but not Jerry. Perhaps he was too disgusted.

"Better hop up and get Topthorn settled," Mr Redman told Jerry. "Takes a good half hour to get his back down," he explained to the Bells.

Veronica quickly forestalled the question she saw rising to Mrs Bell's lips.

Harlequin tipped Tony into the open ditch

"Please, Mummy, would you mind fetching our numbers while we get the ponies ready?"

An hour later Harriet and Marigold were doing their dressage test. The arena, marked out in white, seemed smaller than their practice one, and the markers were inexorable. They allowed no margin, such as the choice of two mole hills, when striking into the canter, and Harriet over-ran several. She could imagine the comments being written on her test paper: late change into trot; pony on wrong bend; pony behind the bit.

But what did it matter anyway with the cross-country looming up?

When it was Veronica's turn Smoky made the first circuit crookedly because he was shying at the white line. After that Harriet thought they did rather well except for a ragged halt.

Jerry and Topthorn were next. Jerry's aids were almost invisible and Topthorn's transitions were made dead on the markers. All the time his keen head was looking the way he was going. He looked, indeed, thoroughly at home in the arena.

Veronica and Harriet exchanged envious glances, then went to prepare for the ordeal of the cross-country. This consisted in taking off their coats, collecting their sticks and tightening girths.

The first three obstacles were visible. Then the current pair vanished into the valley from which the wood spread up to the horizon. If they survived the Trakener they could be seen crossing two fields before finally vanishing behind a tall hedge.

Harlequin tipped Tony into the open ditch and then ran off, but Maureen and Squib survived, Squib's bouncing stride easily identifiable as they crossed the fields beyond the wood. Soon Ann reappeared there, but travelling much faster.

At last it was Harriet's turn.

"Good luck!" shouted Veronica, but she hardly heard.

First came an easy rail, then a trimmed-down hedge with no ditch. Marigold jumped them confidently. But two strides from the open ditch she showed alarm. Harriet was prepared.

"Come on, girl," she cried, driving valiantly on.

Marigold took off, but having lost impetus she dragged her legs through the hedge beyond. Her faith thus shaken, she stopped decisively three times before the wood stack. The judge spread his arms wide, and the Event was over so far as Harriet was concerned.

Sad, but not surprised, Harriet retired to a place from which she could watch for Veronica.

Presently there was the sound of hoofs and she came into view, cantering steadily, Smoky's sharp, forward-pointing ears questioned the wood stack, but he did not falter.

"Goody, they're over that!"

But the turn in the cattle-pen was sharper than he liked, and twice he jumped out on the wrong side of the red flag. "Would Veronica have collected him better in a Kimblewick?" wondered Harriet.

At the third attempt they just managed it and cantered on down into the shadow of the wood. Ahead the fresh chip marks on the birch bole glinted threateningly against the cave-like black entrance into the wood.

Smoky looked as if he might make the leap, but at the last moment he slithered to a halt.

Veronica tried twice more, but his mind was made up.

"Out of the way quick," cried the girl on duty. "There is another rider coming."

Jerry and Topthorn came into view, bounding easily over the wood stack. They were travelling fast, yet Topthorn hopped in and out of the pen with the adroit twist of a ballet dancer.

Veronica hustled Smoky out of the way just in time and the pair flew over the Trakener and vanished into the wood with a flicker of shoes.

"They made it look as easy as wink," said Veronica, joining Harriet.

They waited to see Jerry jump out of the wood again farther along. But minutes passed.

"He should be out before this at the pace he was going," observed Harriet.

24

While they wondered another rider arrived, jumped the Trakener after one refusal and reappeared out of the wood. What could have happened to Jerry? They decided to ask the girl judging the Trakener. She was just as puzzled by Jerry's and Topthorn's non-reappearance.

"They were going so strongly," she said. "And there's nothing in the way of an obstacle between this and the jump out of the wood. Could they have hit a tree? I can't leave, but if you went in at that gate higher up you might find out what's happened."

They did as she suggested. They found the two jumps linked by an easy track and no sign of Jerry or Topthorn along it. The pair had completely vanished.

They heard hoofs approaching, but it was another competitor jumping into the wood, appearing to come out of the blue sky. As they swung their ponies out of the way and in among the trees, Veronica pointed out some tracks in the damp leaf mould.

"Those look like Topthorn's."

"Jerry must have gone mad then. He couldn't possibly have missed the way."

"Listen! Shouting!" exclaimed Veronica, hurrying Smoky's cautious, slithering steps.

Someone *was* shouting hoarsely: "Help! Help!"

Then, between some dark alders, they saw Jerry with Topthorn apparently kneeling at his feet.

"Don't bring your ponies any closer," Jerry shouted. "Topthorn's stuck."

They now saw that Topthorn was nearly up to the girth in a bog.

There was nothing for it but to hitch Marigold and Smoky up by the reins. Then, sinking well over their jodhpur boots, they joined Jerry. Topthorn was in a pitiable plight.

By the way both black mud and yellow clay were churned, he had struggled hard to get out before exhausting himself. He lay now with his fine head stretched on the mud looking imploringly up at them.

"He's completely done in," said Jerry, sounding near to tears.

"We'll fetch help, a rope," offered Harriet.

"Or break off some branches and push under him," suggested Veronica.

"Try that," said Jerry. "I couldn't because I was afraid to leave his head in case he went farther in."

Quickly the girls collected a heap of branches and with Jerry's help pushed them in under Topthorn. Seemingly he knew they were helping him. His expression became less hopeless. He raised his head and even munched a spray of leaves. When they had thrust in all the branches they could, Jerry called upon Topthorn to make a great effort to try and drag himself out of the churned-up mud.

"Come on, Toppy! Hup, boy."

In response to this and a pull on the reins, Topthorn heaved and strained. He loosened his front legs and then was able to get some purchase on the boughs. They all began to shout encouragements. The pony wrenched and fought and finally with some nasty gluggling noises got out on to safe ground.

"Gosh, what a mess!" exclaimed Harriet.

Raddled with black and yellow, his plaits dishevelled and his tail a plastered hank, Topthorn was a travesty of the dapper creature who had set out on the journey. His rescuers were not much better.

"But how did it happen?" demanded Veronica. "You couldn't have lost the way."

"Of course not," muttered Jerry. "I just didn't want to finish the course. But I didn't know of the beastly bog."

"But you'd done all the worst jumps," said Harriet.

"I don't care a tick about the jumps. It was because of Topthorn."

"But . . ."

"I'm sick of it." Jerry's words now came tumbling out. "Every time I get a sort of partnership with a pony, *he* sells it. People think it's fine having lots of mounts and being in the money with them. But Toppy's different. I couldn't let him down by making a mess of the dressage or putting him wrong at a jump, so I took the wrong course on purpose to get eliminated."

The conversation with Mr. Redman about Veronica needing a

"Come on, Toppy! Hup, boy."

bigger pony flashed into Harriet's mind.

"Of course! Your father was going to sell Topthorn if he did well today. Now he can't?"

"That's what I thought. Then I was scared stiff when he got in that bog and I thought he was done for, which would be worse than selling him."

"Well, you'll be eliminated all right," comforted Veronica. "Even if you finished you'd be too late."

"This time," said Jerry. "But there'll be another event. It's only put it off and Dad 'll be mad. I should have known it wouldn't work." He turned away and tried to scrape some of the mud off Topthorn with a handful of twigs. Harriet put the question both girls wanted to know.

"But why not tell your father you want to keep Topthorn?"

"He wouldn't understand. We've had better ponies, better performers, I mean, I haven't minded being sold. But Topthorn's different in another way. We're friends. That's what Dad wouldn't understand. He's bought and sold ponies all his life like Grandad before him. He'd think I was bonkers wanting to keep Toppy not because he was that special but just because I—well—loved him."

The pain in Jerry's admission was so great that neither girl knew how they should reply.

As they disentangled their reins from the bush where their ponies had been nibbling, they were aware of an unfair feeling of thankfulness for the homely presences of Marigold and Smoky. Part of the family, as Mrs Bell often called them.

Just then the squelching of feet and sound of voices came through the trees. They heard Mrs Bell say:

"Surely they can't all three be lost?"

A man replied: "That boy's taken leave of his senses."

"Oh, gosh, it's Dad!" said Jerry.

"Well, it's time somebody came and looked for us," observed Harriet.

"How in the world did you get in this pickle?" was Mr Redman's greeting to his son.

"Got stuck in a bog," muttered Jerry.

"Thank goodness they're safe, ponies and all," said Mrs Bell.

"But what were you doing down here?" persisted Mr Redman. As Jerry seemed unable to explain, Veronica did:

"Jerry and Toppy didn't want to be parted so they ran away into the wood. And it's your fault, Mr Redman."

"It's a mistake," Jerry managed to get out.

"Mistake!" shouted Mr Redman. "It's crazy! I'll get to the bottom of this. But first the pony's got to be seen to."

He seized Topthorn's reins and strode off with him, leaving Jerry to stumble after them.

The Bells followed more slowly, Harriet and Veronica giving their mother a vivid account of what had happened. As it was uphill most of the way back, Mrs Bell lacked the breath to do more than exclaim: "Gracious!" from time to time.

When they got to the box Topthorn was wearing a rug and Mr Redman was bandaging his legs. Jerry was sluicing his bridle in a bucket of water. An ominous silence lay between them. But when he had finished bandaging, Mr Redman came to speak to the girls. He was no longer angry but very puzzled.

"I still can't make any sense of Jerry. What did you mean about this being my fault?"

It was now the turn of Veronica and Harriet to be tongue-tied. So Mrs Bell spoke up for them:

"I understand it all happened because Jerry was so upset by the idea of your selling Topthorn. After all, he's not very big, surely the pony would last him for a long time yet?"

"It's not a matter of lasting him," said Mr Redman a little indignantly. "It's just not policy to keep a pony once it's reached its peak. What's got into Jerry to make him act so silly over this animal?"

"It seems perfectly natural to me that children should love their ponies," said Mrs Bell.

Mr Redman looked out of his depth but reconciled.

"Oh, well, if that's how he feels, we'll keep the pony."

Jerry looked up fleetingly from the bucket. He said nothing, but his expression was of pure joy.

Soon after Topthorn was loaded and the Redmans drove away. The Bells had a peaceful picnic tea with Tony and Maureen, or as peaceful as the presence of four ponies anxious to share in the proceedings would allow. They were all staying to the end because Maureen and Squib were through to the show-jumping phase. In the end they came third.

"So we *have* got a rosette for the windscreen," she gleefully informed Mr Pargeter.

"Cor!" said Mr Pargeter. "And I was afraid at one time we were all going to be out of the money."

"I'm glad Maureen won," Veronica said afterwards to Harriet. "Even though it does bear out what I was saying about needing a horsy background. All the same . . ."

"It's not everything," concluded Harriet.

The Noble Cause

by ELIZABETH RIGBEY

I know that skewbalds are reputed to be very unlucky, but my pony Seeker has brought me enough luck to last a lifetime. In fact, our latest adventure started with Seeker. He was loose in the paddock and I was doing the mucking out, when I turned round to see him in the act of swallowing a stinging nettle.

"Seeker!" I yelled. He looked up at me wisely, but carried on eating. By the time I reached him he'd finished it completely.

"Oh help! You'll sting your throat or something drastic. You might even die," I shrieked.

"Why?" asked a calm voice behind me. It was my sister, Carol.

"He's eaten a stinging nettle. What shall I do?" I yelled.

"Oh, I shouldn't think it will hurt him," she replied casually. "But if you're really worried, you'd better go and look through the back numbers of my 'Horse News'. I seem to remember something about stinging nettles."

I rushed off and spent ages searching through back numbers. Eventually I read, under "Letters to the Editor", that stinging nettles were harmless to horses. It was then that my eye caught another letter, entitled "CRUELTY MUST STOP", and I started to read it.

I won't make you all cry by quoting from the letter, but by the time I had read it my heart was pounding away and my throat felt very chokey—I really wanted to cry. Actually, though I don't like to degrade myself, I did.

Of course, Carol and my two brothers, Andy and Bob, had to walk in at that very moment. Everybody crowded round trying to be helpful, as people always do when someone is sobbing away.

I pointed feebly to the letter and everybody tried to read it at once. The next thing I knew we were all howling—well, if not actually howling, we were rather red in the face.

"We've got to do something. We can't call ourselves horse lovers, then just ignore the fact that horses are suffering like this," said Andy sensibly.

It was just about then that I hit on the idea of going to a horse sale and saving some poor, broken-down pony from its doom.

"That's an absolutely whizzo idea," exclaimed Bob.

"Wouldn't it be noble of us?" I said enthusiastically. "Perhaps they'll give us medals or something." I was getting rather carried away, but I shut up quickly as everyone gave me withering looks.

"At least living here at Hodbridge Vale gives us enough room to keep an extra pony. There are fields and stables and any amount of hay and straw," pointed out Carol.

"Up Hodbridge Vale Farm," we said automatically, as we always do whenever the farm is mentioned.

"All that remains now is to talk the Pater round to our way of thinking," said Andy.

I don't know how it is that we call Dad "the Pater"—I think it's Latin.

"Adults NEVER think like us," sighed Bob. Although he was immediately ticked off by Carol, who likes to think she *is* an adult, I inwardly agreed with him.

"No," said Dad.

"How noble it would be to rescue a pony from its doom," I said.

"And how humane you'd feel," put in Carol.

"I've said no," answered Dad.

Our last resort was the tear-stained Letter to the Editor, which Andy thrust into Dad's hand. We all tried to see his face as he read it, in case he was suddenly overcome with emotion.

As we had thought, "CRUELTY MUST STOP" did the trick. Although he did not actually burst into tears, he looked very sad, and finally said, "You kids put years on me. Okay, we'll give it a try, but it will have to be one great big Christmas present for all four of you. And you mustn't spend more than £25."

And that was how we came to be standing apprehensively at the November sale, cold and wet, but full of high hopes. "At last we are doing something for the noble cause of equitation," I thought, and though this wasn't strictly true, it made me feel good.

We all looked very conspicuous amongst the farmers and the horse-dealers, sitting astride our ponies in our riding macs. I felt especially small, as I was swamped inside Andy's cast-off mac and the sleeves were about twice as long as my arms.

All manner of horses were led up for auction, prancing ones, plodding ones, youngsters—all sorts of breeds, all shapes and sizes. We had very much wanted to see them all beforehand but, partly because Carol insisted on keeping us waiting while she put on "just enough make-up to make me look sophisticated" and partly because I couldn't find my riding mac, we arrived too late to do so. As each horse was led up we stared at it critically. The trouble was that none of them looked hard done by, and it was a really ruined pony we were looking for.

Behind me were two burly farmers, discussing each horse.

"Old Peter's got rid of that nag at last then," said one.

"They say he's selling up, to move up North."

"Not a bad horse that. I'd go sixty-five, knowing what sort of home it came from."

"There's Lord Myre's head groom. I'm interested in the black mare he's leading. I'll just go and have a word with him. Hold on for me here, Bill."

I slipped on the muddy ground

After listening to their conversation, I simply had to see who Bill was. I tried to turn inconspicuously on the spot (I was standing by Seeker now, holding a cloth over his saddle to keep it dry). Unfortunately, I slipped on the muddy ground and went ploughing straight at Bill.

What a fool I felt, apologising for almost knocking him over! However, he smiled and said cheerfully, "What are you doing in this God-forsaken place?"

Actually, as it was buzzing with farmers and horsy looking men in breeches, it looked anything but a God-forsaken place—but I was far too polite to say so. Instead, I burst out before I could stop myself, "In the noble cause of equitation, we want to find a horse that is broken down and stop it from going to its inevitable doom."

Of course, the minute I had said it I felt a fool, and wished I hadn't.

Bill just smiled broadly and said, "Well, in that case, can I recommend lot number 162 to you? If you want to do something noble, you could buy that skeleton of a horse and watch him getting better and better every day. He will do, sure as beans is beans, at the right sort of home."

"Thank you very much," I gasped. "I'll tell the others. Now. This minute." Which I did.

"Trust you to go burbling away about the noble cause of equitation," said Andy. I could tell he was pleased though.

We walked slowly round to the stalls, leading the ponies. It didn't take us long to find number 162. I felt like crying, the poor horse was so pathetic. He drooped his neck and dragged each leg when he walked, as if it weighed a ton. His coat was scurfy; and patched and matted with thick, clotting mud.

I think that we all decided, within a split second, that 162 was the horse on whom we would bestow our benevolence. I patted him and he looked steadily at me as though I had hit him. I felt like a criminal and hurried away with the others, back to our places.

Suddenly Andy nudged me, I was in the middle of a daydream. Being led up was 162, looking even more pathetic than when we

The poor horse was so pathetic

first saw him.

"Fifteen," said someone feebly.

"Eighteen?" the auctioneer asked hopelessly.

Someone near me nodded.

"Twenty." It was the meat man, I felt sure.

"Twenty-two? Thank you, sir. Going . . . going . . . gone."

It was Andy. Thank heavens he had kept his head and taken everything in his stride. 162 was ours.

The return journey was one long plod. I truly believe that from the time we left the sale to the time we arrived within sight of the house, all we did was plod in a dull, methodical way. We talked too, about the pointless things people talk about in the rain, when they are cold and wet. All the time though, in time to the clip-clop of the horses' hooves, the words "the noble cause of equitation" kept drumming through my head.

Suddenly Bob, who keeps getting asked to join the school choir and keeps refusing, burst into the roaring strains of "John Brown's Body", and soon we were singing away (in our not so school choirish voices). Even 162, who, until now, had been the worst plodder of all, pricked up his ears.

The rain stopped and the sun began to reveal more and more of itself from behind a cloud. As we reached the Vale everything looked fresh and new, with sparkling little droplets of rain on every twig and blade of grass. (That makes me sound very poetic—I'm not, really). And soon the strains of "John Brown's Body" were echoing all over Hodbridge Vale and the farm was in sight.

Mopsy (that's our mother—don't ask me why we call her Mopsy, we just always have and we always will) came out to meet us, carrying a nice clean halter to replace the ragged rope one on 162.

"So here's the unsuspecting victim of the Morsworths," she said, deftly changing the halters.

She led 162 into the stable we had prepared for him that morning, with a bed of soft straw and a rack full of sweet smelling hay. The poor, dirty horse made a dive for the hay. For the first time, I could see just a glimmer of contentment in his eyes.

Andy blew an eerie sounding but quite good "Home"

38

After making a hot bran mash and rugging up, Andy said, "A little while ago, I suddenly had the feeling that I could blow the most perfect 'Home' you've ever heard. Shall I try?"

We all urged him to do so. We had acquired a hunting horn from an old friend of Dad's, but, so far, none of us had mastered it. So, standing outside 162's loose box, Andy blew an eerie sounding, but quite good, "Home". When he had finished, 162 flung up his head, and, with a wise look in his tired eyes, whinnied loudly.

Amazingly, the same thing happened again. No other sounds from the hunting horn caused this remarkable change, it only happened when Andy blew "Home".

Eventually we went inside and settled down in the spare room to read or do Pony Club quizzes. It was then that I heard a very familiar voice.

"It's Mr Decker," I yelled, and rushed downstairs.

I had better explain that Mr Decker is the District Commissioner of our Pony Club Branch, and you couldn't find a nicer, more understanding, D.C. anywhere.

"Hallo, Mr Decker," I screeched.

"Hallo, Dorothy. Your father has just been telling me about your latest escapade—and a very good one it is too."

"Oh, you must come and see 162 now, you'll love him. He's so sweet and filthy, and he's got lovely eyes. We haven't groomed him yet. Dad says to let him settle down first." In my enthusiasm, I forgot to be offended about the noble cause of equitation being called an "escapade".

"Call the others then, and I will," said the D.C.

Soon we were all walking back to the stables.

"It's strange," I remarked, "162 whinnies every time we blow 'Home'."

"Funny, I once had a horse who did that—best horse I ever had," said Mr Decker. "I sold him because I thought I was going abroad, and I've regretted it ever since. I'd still know him anywhere."

"You wouldn't know this one. He's so dirty, you can't see him," said Carol.

39

We neared the stable.

"May we present you to . . ." Bob began. But he was suddenly interrupted by a loud excited voice.

"MOONKING!"

We stared at the D.C. in astonishment.

"It's my old horse," cried Mr Decker. I don't think I've ever seen anyone, let alone a D.C., so excited.

"Five years ago," he told us, "I bought a half-broken four-year-old, quite cheaply, but it didn't take me long to see that this horse had great potential. Everyone I knew in the horse world advised me to train him for three-day events. He wasn't just a grand hunter, but a grand everything else, too. He was the most perfect horse I'd ever owned.

"Then I got a letter, telling me to go abroad—I won't bore you with the reason why—so I had to sell all my horses. At the last moment, somebody altered my plans and the whole thing was called off. I tried desperately to find this horse again. Nobody could tell me a thing about his whereabouts, and, from that day to this, I haven't seen him. But now . . ."

"He's only nine then," Andy said.

"That means there's still time for the three-day events," I said, getting as excited as the D.C.

"If I can get him back to what he was, there certainly is," agreed the D.C. "You wonderful kids have done it again."

We all turned bright red at this unexpected praise and I wished the whole Pony Club was there to envy us.

The D.C. had been giving 162 a thorough examination. At last he reported, "All that's wrong with him is lack of food and neglect. It won't take long to see to that. You all know what I'm going to say next," he went on, looking round our blank faces. "I'm going to ask you if I can buy this horse back for whatever you gave for him, plus—yes, plus—and this is only if I can get him back to his former standard—a quarter of all his winnings."

We looked, and felt, uncomfortable.

"Thank you, but £22 is what we gave, and £22 is what we'll get," replied Dad slowly, when Mr Decker told him of his offer. But the D.C. wasn't having that.

"You can't possibly refuse, not after finding Moonking for me." We didn't.

"I'll send the horsebox round for him tomorrow then." The D.C. looked as if he might burst with happiness. So did we all. Even 162 seemed to understand and, in spite of himself, positively radiated —well, as best as a horse can.

"You wonderful kids have done it again"

That Pony Will Have to Go

by NICOLA HERD

Shake, shake, shake; always a bad sign when father rattles his paper at breakfast. "Feed's going up and up," he grumbled. "That pony of yours costs the earth. It wouldn't be so bad if the thing could jump, but look at last week—three knock downs and a refusal. It's got no pop in it at all. It'll have to go!" Shake, shake. "Now the wretched thing's cast a shoe, that'll be another bill from old George."

Nicola crept out, miserable; it was so unfair. Candy did have a jump in her somewhere if only she could find it. A few rosettes would make all the difference to Dad's point of view. She went over to the stable and threw her arms round Candy's neck. "Come on, Candy, my love, we'll just have to sort out the jumping. I know we can!"

Nicky saw that, sure enough, Candy had cast a shoe, and later on George the blacksmith came tottering up the lane in his old van, moaning about what a busy day he'd had—not a single shoe left. "I hope you've got the one she cast." No such luck, of course, and old George went on about how he wouldn't be back for a week. "A week!" thought Nicky. That would miss the next circuit show. "Oh, please," she said, "can't you find one?"

It was then she noticed the old shoe nailed up on the beam over the door, an old gypsy's shoe they always said; some story about a magic symbol stamped into the iron. Nicky wasn't too sure about fitting it on Candy. It might be bad luck, or something. Still, it was that or nothing, and grumbling a bit, George had the nails out of the beam and the shoe down. Not a bad fit, a bit of work with the hammer and anvil from his van and the shoe was on. Candy put her hoof down and pawed once or twice, looking inquisitively and sniffing the strange shoe from over the stable door.

Not many hours later a miserable day had turned from bad to worse. The wind rose, howling and gusting. The grey clouds piled up and whilst Candy and Nicky were on their hack round the lanes, the heavens opened and the rain lashed down; thunder rumbled and lightning started to stab the sky.

Head down in her collar and eyes screwed up, Nicky hunched into the storm and it was Candy who first saw the lightning flash strike down into the big elm, and she caught Nicky unawares as she reared in fright. Nicky hung on instinctively as the pony leapt sideways, and in so doing saved them both from the splintering crunch of the great trunk as it crashed to the ground. As it was, a mass of branches whiplashed down and swept the girl from the saddle. Candy pranced about in the path, shivering and whinnying with fright. She turned and tiptoed up to the figure of Nicky who lay very still on the path in a pattering puddle of water. The pony put a nostril to Nicky's ear and blew—no response. A whinny and a tentative nuzzle. Still no movement. Candy took a nip of the mackintosh sleeve and jerked it gently.

Nicky shook her head and became aware of the noise, the cold, the wet; and that she wasn't in Candy's saddle. She sat up with a splitting head and took in the situation, while Candy towered above her, puffing into her face and trembling with fright. After a couple of attempts Nicky realised she couldn't get up and put her weight on her ankle. Candy was torn between getting out of the storm as fast as she could gallop to the warmth and shelter of her stable, or

The frightened pony clattered into the yard

staying by her young friend with whom there was obviously something very wrong. Nicky knew the pony was her one link with help. "Home, Candy, home and fetch them!" The pony stood undecided, head down, eyes wide. A couple of sniffs and puffs at Nicky and she seemed to get the right idea. She picked her way round the fallen tree and after some hesitation made up her mind and set off.

The frightened pony clattered into the yard, mud spattered, irons flying, and no Nicky. Trouble must have struck the pair. Dad phoned the doctor and then, using the pony as a guide, set off with more of the family to find Nicky.

The doctor had to drive up a winding valley road, passing quite near to where Nicky lay, but on the other bank of a stream, and then cross by the wooden bridge to reach her. The anxious group, who had by now found the girl, watched the doctor drive through the rain, and then slither to a halt at the edge of the bridge, which the horrified onlookers could see had collapsed under the torrent of rushing water which replaced the usually gentle stream. The doctor reversed his car along the bank opposite them, but though they yelled and waved to each other the storm made even a shouted conversation impossible.

It was then that Candy took matters into her own hands. She swung in a tight circle, and cantered for the stream, took off and cleared it, landing in a splatter of turf on the far bank to the incredulous disbelief of the family; none of them would have thought Candy had a pop in her like that! Nickering urgently, she pushed the doctor towards the bank—but he couldn't jump it! Yet, perhaps with help? Measuring the pony and the gap with his eye, he hesitated a moment; he hadn't been in a saddle for years. Then, snatching up his bag, he swung into her saddle and before he had a chance to think better of it, she took off again for the other side. Hanging on to pony and bag, they landed inelegantly but safe, and the doctor got to work.

Some days later when Nicky's ankle was mending they noticed that Candy had cast a shoe again. Once more George rattled up the drive in his van, and the family gathered round to tell him the story. While they chatted it was George who happened to glance up over the stable doorway and noticed the old gypsy shoe: cobwebbed and in exactly its old spot—as if it had never been moved.

"Well, I'll be . . . !" he said.

George noticed the old gypsy shoe

Jennifer's Pony

by CDR. H. FALCON-STEWARD

It was a glorious sunny morning, the countryside was coming to life after a dreary winter. Flycatcher was on his toes and I reproved him as he shied foolishly when a blackbird flew out of the hedge. As we rounded a corner in the lane I saw a small figure on a pony coming towards us and recognised Jennifer. I reined in, but instead of the usual bright vivacious girl, Jennifer could hardly raise a smile.

"Hello, young lady," I said. "Why so glum on such a lovely morning?"

"This is our last ride," she said. "Moonbeam has been put in the sales tomorrow."

"Oh dear," I said, "that is sad, What has happened?"

"We are moving into Apple Tree Cottage next week and there won't be anywhere to keep Moonbeam, and anyhow Mum says that we won't be able to afford to keep a pony now." She was on the verge of tears.

"Well, cheer up," I said, "things are never quite as bad as they seem." A stupid remark, but what could be worse than a young girl being parted from her beloved pony. I left it at that and rode on. An unhappy child distresses me very much.

All the village had been shocked when Jennifer's father had been killed in an accident three months earlier. He had been a good tenant farmer at a small farm a few miles away and it had been easy enough to keep a pony for Jennifer. Although the farm sale had been good I knew that Jennifer's mother would not find things easy and there would be little to spare after the purchase of Apple Tree Cottage, certainly not enough to afford the luxury of a pony. Besides, as Jennifer had said, there would be nowhere to keep it.

It was a tragedy, and would be a double tragedy if the Pony Club Branch were to lose Jennifer and her pony. Although I had handed over as District Commissioner two years earlier, I had kept in touch and I knew that Jennifer was the mainstay of the Prince Philip Cup team. She was a dedicated rider and she lived for her pony.

Although not in the show pony class, Moonbeam was one of the most generous ponies I had ever known; a first class 'all-rounder". She had gone from strength to strength with Jennifer and the thought that they were to be parted was unbearable. Something must be done. I rode on deep in thought until Flycatcher reminded me that this was no way to enjoy a spring morning, so I turned into the thirty acres and let him out across the springy turf. This must have cleared my brain for by the time we arrived home it was clear what had to be done.

I went into my study and searched for the sales catalogue on my desk. There is was: Lot 79, Moonbeam 13.2 hh bay mare, 8 years. Quiet to handle, box and shoe etc., a first class child's pony. Genuine reason for sale. And that, I thought, is an understatement.

I did not know if I would be able to get over to the sales in time but I was pretty certain that Jack would be there. He bred some good ponies and usually had one or two animals in the sale. I gave him a ring.

"Jack," I said, "are you taking any ponies to the sales tomorrow?"

"Sure," he said, "I've got two very promising three year olds which ought to do quite well."

"Well, look, I don't know whether I shall be able to get over in time, but I want you to do me a favour. Will you buy Lot 79 for me?"

"Lot 79? Just a minute." I could hear him turning the catalogue.

"Here we are, Lot 79, Moonbeam 13.2 hh bay mare . . . What on earth do you want a 13.2 for, have you reached your second childhood?"

"Not quite," I said, "but the Prince Philip Cup is involved."

"Okay," he said, "what's the limit?"

"There isn't one," I said. "I'll bring the trailer over."

Jack mumbled something about being a philanthropist and rang off.

When I got to the sales the ponies were coming in and had reached Lot 74. I stood at the back and spotted Jack in a good position. The next few lots were moderate and made poor prices. Then Moonbeam came in. That pony had presence and, as always, was beautifully turned out. I sensed a stir of interest round the ring.

I heard the auctioneer saying "Lot 79, Moonbeam 13.2 hh bay mare. A genuine all-round child's pony, gentlemen, with a great reputation in the Pony Club, I believe. Will anybody bid me £50? Thank you, sir. £60, £70, £80 to you over there, sir. £90 I'm bid." Jack had come in and bidding was slowing down. Finally Moonbeam was knocked down to Jack for £140. A voice behind me said:

"Gone to a ruddy breeder, some poor kid will miss a good ride."

A good investment, I reflected, and the interest from it was going to be a child's happiness. I wandered off to where the saddlery was being sold. I didn't know what Jennifer had done with her tack but I had a suspicion that Moonbeam needed a new saddle. I managed to acquire a saddle and bridle in good condition at a reasonable price and went off to look for Jack.

"Hope I didn't go too far," he said. "She's a good pony and I wouldn't mind having her in my own yard."

"Thanks a lot," I said. "I agree that she might produce a good foal one day." I gave him my cheque, boxed up and set off for home. Moonbeam was no stranger to my stables and Flycatcher gave a little whinny of welcome as I put her into the box next to him.

Next day I rode over to Apple Tree Farm. The cottage had been sold off separately a few years ago when the need for cottages had diminished; now I wished that it still belonged to me. I sought out Tom.

"Tom," I said, "would it worry you a lot to give up a couple of acres of the twelve acre field behind Apple Tree Cottage?"

Then I explained that Jennifer and her mother were going to live at the cottage and that they would need somewhere for the pony.

"Reckon it won't make much difference," Tom said, "but I heard as how the pony was to be sold."

"Well, it is up at my stables now," I said, "until arrangements can be made."

Tom's two girls were also in the Pony Club and I knew they were friends of Jennifer.

"Well," said Tom, "tell her it will be all right to put the pony in the meadow now until you get the rails up. My two ponies are there and the girls will keep an eye on it."

That evening I wrote to Jennifer:

Dear Jennifer,

I went to the sales today and bought a pony. I thought it would be a good companion for Flycatcher, but now I realize that it will need exercising and I fear that it is not up to my weight. Perhaps you would like to ride it for me? If you are not too busy moving house at the weekend come up to my stables and see what you think of it . . .

On Saturday morning I was busy in the tack room when I heard steps outside and Jennifer appeared.

"Hello," I said, "come and see my new pony."

We went over to the stables and I opened the door of the loose box.

"Why," she cried, "it's Moonbeam." Flinging her arms round the pony's neck she burst into tears of joy. When she had recovered I suggested that she should tack up and ride home.

"You can put her in Tom's field behind the cottage for the time being until we have railed off a couple of acres. Later on we'll fix up a shelter. To all intents and purposes she is your pony but I will

Flinging her arms round the pony's neck she burst into tears of joy

provide the fodder if you will look after her for me. In a few years you will outgrow her and then perhaps she will have a foal."

I saw them out of the yard and was conscious of a great joy. "Take care," I said, "she has not been out for three days." But I knew they would be all right.

Three weeks later I was enjoying my after breakfast pipe when I heard the crunch of hoofs on the gravel outside. I went to the front door. A radiant girl was holding a pony with a red rosette on its bridle.

"You been to a show already, Jennifer?" I said.

"No," she said, "it's the Prince Philip Cup; we're through to the Zone Finals. Isn't it super!"

Then I heard the telephone ringing. It was Dick, the District Commissioner.

"Have you heard our news?" he said. "We've got into the Zone Finals and I gather we have you to thank for Jennifer still having a pony."

"The little so and so," I said, "she promised she wouldn't tell."

"Oh, it wasn't Jennifer," said Dick. "I met Jack last night and he said something about you having reached your second childhood and wanting to ride in the Prince Philip Cup. Then the penny dropped. The Branch is delighted but I think it's you who deserves a reward."

"I've got it," I said. "It's outside the front door at the moment; I've never seen such a picture of happiness."

A Promise to Dawn

by VERONICA RICHES

"I've washed your jodhpurs and put them in the airing cupboard," Mum told me as I sat down to tea. "You won't forget to pack them in the morning, will you?"

"Thanks, Mum," I replied. "Do you know, I'm getting quite nervous about it. I mean, some of the kids I'll be teaching are only a year or two younger than I am and they may think that I'm being awfully bossy."

"No they won't; they know you're just trying to help them," Mum reassured me. "You didn't think your instructress was bossy when you were at Pony Club Camp last year, did you? And she looked very young to me; she couldn't have been more than eighteen or nineteen. Besides, the D.C. wouldn't have asked you to instruct if he hadn't thought you capable."

"Actually Deborah is only just eighteen now, but she's had so much more experience than I've had." In my mind's eye I pictured Deborah Berkley-Hope—tall, slim, fair-haired and always in command of the situation. She never froze into uncomfortable silences when thrust among the 'horsy set'; she always knew which horses were in the money, the horses up for sale, the riders in search of a good horse. She never looked nervous, tired or dishevelled; she was just one of those terribly capable people.

"Experience doesn't necessarily count," Mum said, handing me a cup of tea. "A brilliant scientist may be a very poor teacher, whereas someone with only a very basic knowledge of the subject may be an excellent teacher. It's just a matter of personality. Anyway, I think you'll be a very good teacher, you've done a lot of preparation for the lessons and you've a nice clear voice and you've . . ."

"Oh Mum, don't!" I said. Being praised was so embarrassing, especially as I was not sure that I deserved it. True, I had made a list of ideas for lessons, but as for my voice—well, it always became very high and squeaky when I was nervous.

"It'll soon be dark," I said. "I'd better go and feed Dawn."

"Nicky?"

I saw the look in Mum's eyes and I knew what was coming.

"Nick, I know we've been through this before, but surely you realise that if you don't sell Dawn you will be virtually giving up riding. Daddy just cannot afford to keep another horse. And you seem to be growing taller by the day; it won't be long before you can tie your legs in a knot under her tummy. Think of all the opportunities you're missing! If you agreed to sell Dawn we would be able to buy you a bigger horse and you'd be able to participate in things so much more."

"You just don't understand," I said hotly. I could feel the tears gathering behind my eyes, the familiar knot tightening at the base of my throat. Nobody, not even my own mother, was able to understand my feelings for Dawn.

"But, Mum," I pleaded, "she's nearly seventeen years old. I know she doesn't show her age because she is such a gay little pony but I'm terribly careful with her just the same. If someone else had her, they wouldn't know her as I do, they might gallop her around and get her all fizzed up like she was when I first had her. Anyway, I can still hack her out quietly and, what is more, I LOVE her."

Mum sighed and resignedly began to clear away the tea things. "All right, but I'm sure there are lots of people who would give her a very good home."

I went out then, slamming the door behind me in an effort to disperse my emotion, and wandered down to the shed to mix Dawn her feed. At the sight of me, she neighed and cantered towards the gate, splashing me with mud as she came skidding to a halt.

"Dear old Dawn," I flung my arms around her neck and buried my face in her thick chestnut mane. "Don't worry, I promise that I shall never, never sell you."

The next morning I woke up early. It seemed to me that I had been taking imaginary riding lessons all night long in my sleep and, strangely enough, it stopped me feeling so nervous; I really felt quite an old hand at the game. I ate breakfast and then went out to say goodbye to Dawn. Mum was going to feed her while I was away but I still felt rather a traitor leaving her behind.

"I'm not deserting you," I told her, giving her a carrot—"at least, not in my thoughts."

Then I heard my father calling me from the car and I ran back to the house to collect my suitcase.

We got lost on the way to the camp site and I was so hot and bothered I wanted to chicken out of the whole ordeal. But when we eventually did arrive, nobody seemed to have noticed that I was nearly an hour late. Dad unloaded my case and then rushed off as he would be late for work. I noticed Deborah leading a horse out of a stable and I hurried over to speak to her. At least she might be able to tell me what I was supposed to do.

"Hello, Nicola. I hear you're instructing this year," she greeted me. "By the way, you've got my sister on your ride; this is her horse. Make sure you're firm with her, won't you? She's terribly soft and allows Astronaut to get away with murder. Nice horse, don't you agree?"

"Mmmm, he is nice," I replied. Deborah's self-assurance had the power to wipe all intelligent remarks from my mind, so that I usually ended up conversing in mono-syllables.

I took a deep breath and spluttered on. "Er . . . Deborah, do you know where I'm supposed to go? The first lesson starts at ten o'clock, doesn't it?"

"Yes. Your school is over there." She pointed to a circle at the far end of the field. "Actually, you could take Astronaut over to my sister; she's over by the school. She came off him as we were riding over this morning but she should be O.K. by now. Thanks awfully! See you later."

I took Astronaut, a smart grey gelding of fifteen hands and led him over to the school. Most of my ride seemed to have already gathered and the D.C. came over and introduced me to them. He told us that there would be a period of instruction each morning and then a lecture and a ride out in the afternoons. He also told me that I was to be lent a horse from the local riding school for the rides out and that on the last day of camp there would be a show, with prizes for the groups gaining most points during the week. Then he left us to get on with the lesson.

Mum had been right. No one in my ride resented my telling them what to do and I really enjoyed teaching them. The only problem was Astronaut. Helene, Deborah's sister, was clearly petrified of him and spent most of her time on the verge of tears. He was just too full of himself and at the slightest excuse would either leap forward or stop dead with a snort. I suggested to Helene that she should put him on the lunge early in the mornings, which she did, and although it helped slightly it was obvious that he was too big and strong for her. The inevitable disaster happened while we were out riding on the third afternoon of camp.

It was a hornet's fault. Its buzzing had made Astronaut fidgety and I think in the end it must have stung him, because all of a sudden he shot by us at a flat-out gallop with a terrified Helene tugging at his reins.

"Oh no!" I heard Deborah yell. "That track leads to the main road."

"We can cut across the fields," I shouted, already urging my horse through a gap in the hedge. "Come on, horse! Come on! Come on!" We raced across the field, through an open gate and into a field of potatoes. The going was very heavy and my horse began to slow but I drove him on relentlessly, the vision of the main road looming

It must have stung him

large in my mind. "Come on! Please, please, come on!" As I neared the hedge bordering the track, I could see Astronaut approaching from the left. Helene was no longer aboard and from the mud plastered to his side it was obvious that he had been down.

The gate into the lane was shut. I shortened my reins and urged my horse straight for the hedge. I am not a brave person but, faced with no alternative but to jump, I just did not have the time to be frightened. With a grunt my horse heaved himself out of the mud, we seemed to be going through rather than over the hedge as brambles caught and tugged viciously at my clothes, but the good old horse had his blood up and miraculously we scrambled out on to the track the other side. Astronaut was only a few yards off but already slithering to a stop. I slipped to the ground, my knees quaking, and he meekly allowed me to catch hold of his reins.

That all happened four months ago but I can remember it as though it were yesterday. I had only just caught Astronaut when the rest of the riders came into sight. Helene had not been badly hurt but she was shocked and kept screaming that she never wanted to ride again, so Deborah had to telephone from a nearby house to ask her mother to come and collect her.

Astronaut was very lame and the next day the vet said that he had strained a tendon and would have to be rested for three months. Well, after that, things soon settled down again and the rest of the week at camp flew by. Deborah's ride won the Points Cup for the week with my ride a close second and the D.C. awarded me the cup for having the group showing most improvement in their riding.

It was nice to be back home again and have Dawn but somehow it seemed rather an anti-climax after camp. I took Dawn out for the occasional ride along the lane but I felt so enormous on her that I would get off and walk for most of the way. One day when I was leading Dawn, I met Deborah out riding on one of her show jumpers. We chatted for a while and she even slid off her horse to walk alongside me. She had been different since the accident, but I was still surprised when she told me how nervous she was about going off to college in France that coming weekend. I asked her about Helene and Astronaut and she said that her parents were still trying to persuade Helene to ride him again.

"Surely it would be better for her to start riding again on a quieter horse," I suggested. "She can always come and ride Dawn if she likes; I'm getting too big to give her enough exercise."

Well, Deborah didn't remark on my suggestion but the next day I received a telephone call from her mother, Mrs Berkley-Hope, inviting me over for tea that afternoon. Of course I agreed, and immediately started fussing around wondering what to wear. But, to my surprise, Deborah's parents turned out to be quite homely and not in the least overpowering. Over tea, we talked about horses in general and then got on to the subject of Dawn.

"We have an idea which we hope may appeal to you," Mrs Berkley-Hope said with a smile. "Helene has told us how much you helped her with her riding at camp. You are more patient than Deborah, and when she heard of your kind offer to give her lessons on your own pony she absolutely leapt at the idea. Now, dear, we were hoping that maybe you'd be willing to help us a little further." She paused a moment and I wondered how on earth I could be expected to help the Berkley-Hopes.

"Astronaut," she said with a sigh, "is positively bursting out of his skin and yet there is nobody to ride him. Ridiculous, isn't it? I thought that perhaps we could interest you?"

Interest! That was the understatement of the year.

It's all been settled! Astronaut is arriving tomorrow. He's going to live with Dawn so that Helene and I can ride out together. The Berkley-Hopes are going to supply all the feed and hay as they still insist that I am doing them a favour. And, what is more, when Helene is ready to ride Astronaut again they said they would love to have Dawn to stay, to act as a steadying influence on their young show jumpers. It's like a dream; my parents are going to buy me a bigger horse and although I shall not see her so often, I will not have broken my promise to Dawn.

A Polo Conversation

by PAULINE GERRARD

Clopper-clop, clopperty-clop, clop-clop. Big, bay, lumbering Shire-like Leo, with his shaggy mane, feathered legs and plates of feet, stepped unevenly but enthusiastically down the pot-holed tarmac drive to the farm. He was wondering, as he tugged at his bit, if there was going to be some polo after all, because this is where it all started for him the year before. So when he was untacked and turned into the paddock with the ponies who lived on the farm, he was all for enquiring about the polo; but of course they had to get their preliminary horsey introductions over first.

Wizard, the Welsh pony, was nearest to him. Leo trotted up to his old acquaintance who stood waiting with arched neck, the white blaze on his face a definite contrast to his brown body and legs. Wizard flashed a white-socked foreleg at the approaching Leo, who stopped dead once their noses were touching. "'Allo", "'alloo" they both squealed to each other, turned a complete circle in opposite directions, touched noses and squealed again.

Tall, rakish, all-thoroughbred Grouse cantered sedately up to them. He stood next to Wizard, their profiles merging; they were the

He was wondering if there was going to be some polo after all

same colour except that Grouse was devoid of any white. His "How-do-you-do" squeal sounded rather hollow, as if he had woken up with a sore throat that morning, but he had not, he always spoke like this nowadays since he had been hobdayed.

Winston, whose mother was a Welsh-cross arab and father was a thoroughbred, was rather more finely bred than either Leo or Wizard. He joined the others just as they began the next stage of the horsey introductions, a gallop to the end of the paddock. Wizard dropped his head and put in an almighty buck, Winston changed legs as he changed direction, Grouse did a perfect pirouette on his haunches and led the gallop to the other end of the paddock. Leo followed.

Eventually, they all stood quietly, head to tail, flicking the flies from each other's faces. It was Wizard who started the conversation. "Why has that vicar brought you here again?" he wanted to know from Leo.

"He's taken the family away for a few days, so your folk are looking after me," said Leo, adding hopefully, "I thought there might be some more polo."

Grouse neighed in that funny voice of his and said, rather snootily, "Why do you think there should be polo for you? You're not the right sort of pony at all, Leo; you should be pulling a cart or a plough."

"No one in the Pony Club seemed to agree with your sort of thinking," said Leo, slightly aggrieved.

"Leo was really very good," Winston defended. "The man who took us in his lorry last year had a go on him, just sticking and balling, and said he was a real honest pony the way he put his heart into the game when he hadn't done it before and couldn't know anything about it."

"It was real good fun," Leo chuckled, "much better than the odd gymkhana."

"Why did they take you?" Grouse asked.

"Sarah took him instead of me," Wizard sulked. "She said I was getting hard to stop."

"And were you?" Grouse kept probing.

"Not for her."

"Maybe it was because of the way you behaved with that American the year before," Winston suggested.

"Why should that be? It's the way I behave with everyone else, and she knows it."

"What happened then?" Leo asked.

Winston could see that Wizard was not forthcoming, so he began the story himself. "That year there was a team of American students over here—I think they were from one of the best universities—and they played some of the teams in the senior tournament. Of course they hadn't any ponies, so on the first day they borrowed some of the ponies of the children who were playing in the junior tournament. One of our children lent Elf and she played very well for them. Now it was for obvious reasons that Sarah didn't lend Wizard."

Wizard turned his head away, trying to assume an air of boredom; he really didn't see why Winston should keep on so. Winston continued: "The next day the Americans played the Irish Guards on the best pitch. The Irish Guards could only lend the Americans six horses, so unless they could borrow two more they couldn't play the match straight off as there wouldn't be enough ponies to change for each chukka.

"They kept asking over the loud-speaker if anyone in the Pony Club would lend them two ponies for the match. Eventually Mrs Geer, who was in charge of us that year, went to the American manager and told him they could borrow Wizard and Darwin if they liked. I did hear her say, 'You won't thank me for it, but there are two ponies if you feel it necessary to have them.'

"Well," Winston took a breath, "the Americans did thank her for it in a very nice letter some days afterwards, but Darwin and Wizard only lasted one chukka. Both the players used spurs. If spurs are used on Darwin he just stands still and bucks, and anyone can

Darwin had all four feet firmly planted on the ground

guess what happens with Wizard. Mrs Geer did try to warn the Americans that Wizard was no problem to get going, but only a problem to stop. Only she said she didn't like to teach her grandmother how to suck eggs. Those students knew a great deal more about polo than she did."

"Yes," interrupted Grouse, "but they didn't know a lot more about Wizard."

"No," Winston continued, "because halfway through the first chukka the American got off Wizard and took his spurs off. He remounted and joined in the game. Darwin's rider kept his spurs on and, as the game galloped up the field, Darwin had all four feet firmly planted on the ground. Then the play turned the other way and the field started coming towards Darwin. Wizard suddenly noticed him a long way off, so he took hold of his bit and did one of his whizzy acts straight across the pitch, overtaking the whole game and galloping straight past Darwin. In fact he almost disappeared, galloping flat out over a polo pitch and a half before the American could stop him. They decided to manage without the Pony Club ponies after that, even though it meant a gap between chukkas."

"Goes to show what I've been saying is right," grunted Grouse, "none of you chaps are really cut out for polo."

"Rubbish, man," Wizard insisted, "it was only because I saw my chance and took it. Sarah can manage me all right, and that other girl who played a chukka on me; I only got across half a polo pitch with her."

"Really," Winston insisted, "the standard of the Old Berks was improving that year. They were the only Pony Club team who were not attached to a polo club, and they were only bottom by two goals again. The trouble was all the other teams had improved too."

"It doesn't matter about being bottom," Leo insisted, "someone's got to be. The thing is to learn about the game, then, if any of them end up playing for the Irish Guards, they'll know something about it."

"Remember when we practised in Farmer Lane's field?" said Wizard. "His cattle had eaten the grass so bare that our children could thwack the balls up quite a long way before they were stopped by a tussock of grass. The man who trained those Vale of Aylesbury teams that always won told our children the ball ran quite well enough, and that if they could play on that field with the ponies they had they could play anywhere."

"That's what the man from Kirtlington said about the gym horse they had to practise their sticking and balling on—if they could hit a ball on that they could hit it on anything."

"He was a good man. I remember when we were practising on the football pitch and Darwin was playing up, the cunning devil, so the man from Kirtlington got on him, determined to make him into a polo pony."

"That's exactly what he did do," interrupted Winston, "but, oh boy, Darwin did try to beat him. I've never seen him buck so much before or since, and we were all astonished at how that man managed to stay on."

"That was the first year we played," said Wizard. "The tournament was at Kirtlington Park, and the Polo Club allowed the Pony Club children to practise on Tuesday and Thursday afternoons in August."

"They practised at Kirtlington after that as well, when the tournament had moved to Windsor," Winston added.

"Didn't do them much good," grunted Grouse, "the Old Berks teams were always bottom."

"So what," said Leo. "They were good sporting children, and when they got those marvellous double orange rosettes with fourth prize written on them they were as pleased as could be. Sarah wanted to keep hers, but she felt she ought to give it to the Vicar. In the end, those kind people gave her a double white rosette with SPECIAL written on it; special for me, see?"

"Nonsense!" Grouse retorted. "Why wasn't there any polo in the Old Berks this year if everyone enjoyed it so much?"

"It's because most of the children who played before have sold their knock-about ponies and bought event horses, which they don't want to risk at polo. It's nothing to do with coming bottom. They found polo as much fun as anything else in the Pony Club. You don't always have to win just to enjoy something, Grouse."

"They weren't *always* bottom," Leo said. "At the end of that season the V.W.H. had a friendly tournament. There were six or seven teams, including two from the Old Berks, and our first team finished in second place."

"That's right," chipped in Wizard, "I was there as well." He and Winston and Leo all looked at each other, for they knew the real reason why the Old Berks first team had come second in that friendly tournament. At the end of the afternoon they had played the Old Berks second team, and managed to get three goals against them, thus pushing themselves into second place on the total goal scoring. But none of them intended to admit the whole truth. Grouse had been so snooty about the Old Berks polo, he could jolly well put the bare results into his disgruntled old pipe and smoke it!

Double Trouble

by CAROL VAUGHAN

"You look awful," said Melissa.

"I look terrifying," corrected Martin, reaching menacingly for his cardboard tomahawk. He and Patrick had painted red and white streaks across their faces, and wore pheasant-feather head-dresses.

Miss Jervens, the local Pony Club organizer, had drilled the five friends in their roles as "Indians" for the County Show, which included a "Western" Ride amongst its varied attractions—the main one was a demonstration of dressage by Monica Fuller, on the Three-Day Event champion, the ex-milk-cart skewbald, Muldoon.

To add "Indian atmosphere" they had painted white patches on the ponies, Patrick's black, Rebel, becoming a piebald, Rosemary's nervous chestnut mare, Tarantella, and Martin's bay, Traveller, skewbalds, and only Barbara's Fancy Fellow, born skewbald and Melissa's Barbados, a glamorous palomino, had been spared. Traveller had managed to get his tail into a bucket of whitewash and had swished a startling pattern all over Martin's bare chest, adding to his alarming appearance.

"They'll think we are a circus when we ride to the show," said Rosemary, a trim Indian maiden in her mother's suede waistcoat, her long, black (wool) plaits braided with coloured ribbons.

"Proper Indian maidens walked," said Patrick loftily. "Only braves had ponies; it's all women's lib, letting you ride at all. You ought to plod along behind your brave's pony!"

"I would have tickled mustang with pointed stick and watched Indian brave biting dust," said Barbara flatly.

"We are all much too early," said Rosemary. "I knew we would be. What are we going to do? Hang about here for an hour, or go to the show and frighten the spectators—but that would spoil the surprise."

"Do you think Monica Fuller will be giving Muldoon a work-out this morning?" asked Melissa. "They are staying with Mrs Ffrench-floss, aren't they? Perhaps we could go and watch. Felicia was carrying on about it last time I saw her. You'd think *she* was the Three-Day Event champion, to hear her."

Hearing hooves, Martin peered over the hedge and groaned. "You can ask her. Here she comes."

Felicia Ffrench-Floss, whose opinion of her riding ability was shared by no one except her mother—who spared no expense to mount her daughter on the best horses money could buy—was the most unpopular member of the local Pony Club branch.

"I say," said Felicia, reining in her elegant grey mare, Lady Luck. "It's jolly lucky I caught you. Something awful's happened!"

"It's all been cancelled," said Patrick in sepulchral tones. "I saw it in the tea-leaves this morning—disaster, disaster, disaster!"

"You all drink coffee in your family," said Rosemary prosaically.

"Stop being so silly," said Felicia impatiently. "It's important. Muldoon has disappeared. The stable door was wide open this morning. The groom and I have searched all the home paddocks, but he's not there. Monica Fuller's frantic. Miss Jervens came to see her. She told me to try to catch you, to tell you to go to the show by different routes, covering as much ground as possible, in case he has just strayed."

"I've only seen him in photographs," said Melissa.

"It shouldn't be difficult," said Rosemary. "He's a skewbald, close

Felicia rode off beside Patrick

to 16 h.h.—there can't be that many around."

"Let's split into teams of two," said Patrick. "We can cover more ground that way. Felicia, you had better come with me," he added resignedly. He knew, from experience, that she did not get on with any of the girls and Martin always teased her until she lost her temper. "I suggest that Martin and Barbara team up, and Melissa and Rosemary. That gives us three directions to cover."

The next few minutes were a heated geographical discussion on routes and likely places.

"We had better start," said Rosemary. "There isn't that much time. Good luck!"

Felicia rode off beside Patrick, smirking at the other girls, triumphant that Patrick had chosen *her* as his partner, much too conceited ever to guess the real reason. They had a short canter along a lane and came out on the Blasted Oak Heath—named after a lightning-struck tree.

"We had better separate and search each side of it," said Patrick, glad to have a respite from Felicia's tiresome chatter—always about herself. "We'll meet at the ford."

"All right," said Felicia importantly. "I bet I find him."

Patrick kept Rebel to a hand canter, keeping a sharp watch for any movement—a brown and white horse under the trees lining the common would be camouflaged by leaf shadow—watching, too, Rebel's ears, a sure sign if the pony spotted something unusual. His feathered head-band slipped and he pushed it up impatiently; he grinned, wondering what he looked like, with painted face, feathered-head and a moth-eaten moleskin waistcoat flapping over his bare chest.

There was a noise in the trees to his left and Rebel threw up his head, snorting. Patrick reined in. He thought he saw something move. Was that a cry, a distant cracking of branches? Turning, he rode towards the trees, Rebel advancing with the cautious gait of a horse ready to swing round and bolt if it sees danger.

"Muldoon!" exclaimed Patrick, in surprise. "That must have been the thief, running for it, that I heard."

The large skewbald horse was standing under a tree, a halter rope swinging free under its chin; there was no sign of the person who had cried out. Riding forward, talking reassuringly, Patrick grabbed at the halter rope; the horse looked at him curiously.

"Come on, Muldoon," said Patrick, turning and riding back to the heath. "That was easy enough. You'll be at the show in plenty of time."

Cantering down the slope to the ford, Patrick heard a loud whinny, and laughed. So Felicia was already at the rendezvous, after her fruitless search. What a surprise for her!

Reaching the clearing, Patrick reined in with a jerk. Felicia was waiting—holding an identical skewbald.

"I've found . . ." began Felicia importantly, but then, squinting against the sunlight through the leaves, she saw Patrick's skewbald. "Where did you get that one?" she asked. "*I* found Muldoon by the river. I don't understand . . ."

Patrick began to laugh. "But which *is* Muldoon? One of us has pinched someone else's horse."

"Mine's Muldoon," said Felicia crossly; she had been picturing herself as the heroine of the hour.

"I'll toss you for it," said Patrick. "Short of holding an impromptu Three-Day Event, I don't see how we can decide. Come on, to the Police Tent at the County Show. Let's hope they'll have a horsy Sherlock Holmes to sort it out."

Martin and Barbara rode for so long without seeing a single horse that Barbara finally said she thought there had been a clean sweep by the horse-thieves; it wasn't only Muldoon they had taken!

"Don't be an ass, they are all at the show," said Martin.

"Oh, I hadn't thought of that," said Barbara, feeling foolish. "I wonder if the others have had any luck?"

"We shan't know that until we reach the show—unless we find Muldoon," said Martin. "I wonder if there's a reward . . ."

"Look!" said Barbara.

A gypsy encampment on the scrap of wasteland was surrounded

by grazing horses and ponies, some tied up, some hobbled. The big skewbald was standing by the hedge, leaning over the ditch to nibble at the leaves, his halter rope swinging from a broken branch.

"I say," breathed Martin. "Nobbled by the gypsies! What a scoop for us! How are we going to rescue him?"

"We should fetch the police," said Barbara nervously.

"What, and have them spirit away the horse before we get back?" asked Martin impatiently. "You know how clever gypsies are with horses; he'd be dyed brown and in the next county before the local policeman had finished filling in a report. We have to take him now—he's already broken loose, so he's technically a stray—Monica Fuller needs him this afternoon, not next week."

"But that's stealing," squeaked Barbara.

"Nonsense," said Martin. "It's reclaiming lost property. Quite different."

"But we can't just walk up and take him. Someone in those caravans would be sure to notice," objected Barbara.

"I have a plan," said Martin. "Remember, we're Indians. I'm going to crawl up that ditch, grab the halter rope and crawl back, very slowly, towing the horse behind me, keeping his head down, as if he's grazing. You hold the ponies in that lane, ready for the getaway. At the end of the lane there is a little copse, off to the left, leading up to the Market Hill road, the quickest way to the showground."

Barbara shuddered with horror, her mouth dry, but she was not going to let Martin say that girls were useless in emergencies. Starting at every sound, the distant rattle of a saucepan in a caravan, the irritable bark of a dog, the snort of a horse, she waited while Martin slithered off down the lane, feathers rippling down his back. Some ten minutes later Martin suddenly appeared, running, dragging a reluctantly trotting Muldoon behind him.

"Quick," he said. "One of the men has just come out of the caravan. I think he saw . . ." Thrusting the halter rope into her hand, he grabbed Traveller's reins and vaulted into the saddle with a lithe grace any Red Indian might have envied, war-whooping and hitting Muldoon on the rump with the flat of his hand, as there was an angry shout at the end of the lane.

"He's seen us!" choked Barbara, clinging on for dear life as Fancy Fellow shot off down the lane, his ears back, snapping at the galloping skewbald beside him, all three of them all-but bolting.

"He's after us; he's got one of the other horses,"·shouted Martin.

"Quick, turn for the copse; we'll jump the stile and hope he doesn't see where we turned off."

Barbara gulped, wishing herself anywhere else, pulling Fancy Fellow's head round to the sharp turn, dragging Muldoon behind her. The stile loomed ahead. Fancy Fellow's ears pricked; he gathered himself to jump. Muldoon balked and the halter rope slid painfully through her fingers, almost pulling her out of the saddle, so that she jumped with an exaggerated backward seat, like an old-fashioned sporting print, but Fancy Fellow, a solid pony, cleared the obstacle in spite of her and they were flying through the copse. Behind her there was a loud shout and a crash and then Muldoon was racing up beside her. Reaching out, she caught the halter rope. Risking a glance behind her, she could see no sign of Martin—but perhaps he had taken the other path through the copse, to mislead the pursuit.

Reaching the heavy gate onto the road, Barbara dismounted and led Fancy Fellow and Muldoon through, holding it open for Martin, in case the gypsy was still in close pursuit.

Martin appeared quite suddenly through the trees, holding Traveller to a collected trot, a large skewbald horse trotting at his side.

Barbara's eyes widened. "Where did you get that one?" she gasped. "Martin! You can't steal *all* the skewbald horses in the county. You'll be in prison for years. They can't *both* be Muldoon!"

Martin gaped in amazement. "I thought it was the same one," he said, "I thought it had got away from you. When it didn't jump with you, I shouted and it took off from a standing start and went over, but that put off Traveller. I had to put him at it again, and I took the other path, just in case you had missed Muldoon. And I found him.

"Where did you get that one?"

At least, I thought I had."

"Let's go quickly to the police station," said Barbara weakly. "This sort of thing makes me nervous. I don't like being on the wrong side of the law!"

"We are not on the wrong side," said Martin defensively. "We are rescuing Muldoon."

"How many Muldoons are there?" asked Barbara.

"If we find him it'll be a triumph for the superiority of the female brain," said Rosemary.

"I don't feel very superior," said Melissa. "I was always hopeless at all those guessing games we had to do when we went to children's parties; you always won everything."

"Reason it out," said Rosemary, ignoring this. "Two things could have happened. He has strayed or he has been stolen. Which is the most likely!"

"You tell me," said Melissa resignedly. It was never any good interrupting Rosemary's thought processes.

"If he has been stolen by professionals, he is miles away in a horse-box," said Rosemary. "And we shall never find him, but if he has only strayed, he might have been shut in a field by a helpful passer-by, or 'rescued' by a kind old lady, or stolen by a local thief . . ."

This list of solutions seemed endless, but when they reached the main Market Hill road, after an exhaustive search all along their route, they had seen no skewbald horse. . . .

A police car swept past them and stopped on screeching tyres. Tarantella danced backwards, snorting nervously; Rosemary leant forward to pat her neck bringing up a cloud of dried whitewash.

"There they are! Indians! What did I tell you? Officer, arrest them at once!" cried a large lady in magenta slacks and a yellow shirt, bursting out of the police car. "Frightening my poor little Amanda, attacking her, stealing our horse . . ."

"Now then," said Sergeant Jenkins, of the Market Hill police. "What's all this? This lady, Mrs Farringdon-Smith, says her horse was stolen by Indians from a copse off Blasted Oak Heath. I had some difficulty in believing her, but now . . ." He paused, taking in their "fancy dress" with a twinkle in his eye. "It's Melissa Green and . . . Rosemary Straker, isn't it! I know the ponies. Now what's been going on?"

Rosemary and Melissa exchanged glances and began to giggle. That seemed to enrage Mrs Farringdon-Smith even more; she gobbled at them like a turkey.

"We . . . we haven't been near the Heath," said Rosemary truthfully. "Er . . . what colour was the horse?"

"It was a brown and white horse, like something out of a circus," cried Mrs Farringdon-Smith. "I hired it with a gypsy caravan for a week to take the kiddies for a holiday and Amanda begged to be allow to lead it to the river for a drink. And what happens? She is attacked by a horrible Red Indian and comes screaming back to the caravan to fetch her brother, Adrian. But when he goes to look, the horse has gone. And the Indian."

Sergeant Jenkins sighed. "First two circus horses are reported missing, after the road accident to the horse-box—one had to be destroyed, broke a leg, poor brute, and then Mrs Ffrench-floss reports a champion riding horse strayed or stolen from her stables, and now this. What a day!"

"I am afraid that there has been a slight mistake," said Rosemary. "We were out looking for the champion riding horse, with friends of ours, but I can't understand why . . . why Amanda didn't *say* that it was her horse."

"Well, as to that, she didn't actually *see* the Indian take the horse," said Mrs Farringdon-Smith huffily. "Naturally she was so frightened that she ran away when she saw the Indian."

"So the 'Indian' just found an abandoned horse," said Sergeant Jenkins, his brow clearing.

"But that doesn't change anything," cried Mrs Farringdon-Smith. "I want my horse back. Officer, aren't you going to arrest these . . . savages. They are in the same gang."

"Don't see how I could load the ponies into the police car,

madam," said Sergeant Jenkins, winking at the children.

"You'll find him at the show," said Melissa helpfully. "We are all meeting at the Police Tent."

Sergeant Jenkins roared with laughter. "Doesn't sound much like a gang to me," he said. "We'll be off."

"How could Patrick and Felicia have made such a mistake?" said Melissa.

"If you are looking for a skewbald horse—and you find one, loose—I don't suppose you stop to ask questions," said Rosemary reasonably. "Especially when there is no one to ask!"

"Come on," said Melissa. "There's still hope for us—Muldoon is still missing, if they have found a double . . ."

"A ringer," said Rosemary.

"Don't be so technical," said Melissa. "A double is good enough for me—double trouble!"

Long black plaits swaying behind her, Rosemary led the way along the grass verge of the road to Market Hill, in the wake of the police car, still keeping her eyes open for stray skewbalds.

As they passed a gate a wild cry startled the ponies; Tarantella's plunge nearly unseated Rosemary. A fierce-faced, dark-eyed man, with a mop of untidy black hair, astride a raw-boned chestnut horse, was glaring at them across the gate.

"You young varmints!" he yelled. "Indians! Horse thieves! I'll . . ." But he was speaking to thin air. The two ponies were streaking down the road, needing no urging from their horrified riders. A loud, bellowing roar followed them; Melissa risked a look over her shoulder and gasped.

"Golly, he's coming through the hedge! Quick, Rosemary. He's dangerous! Whatever has happened now?"

"I don't know, and I'm not stopping to ask," said Rosemary tersely, all her attention on trying to keep the nervy chestnut mare from bolting. "If we cut across the green at Shepherd's Corner we can jump into the showground over that hedge and hide in the Police Tent. He won't dare to follow us there."

"I'm not so sure," said Melissa, shivering in spite of the blazing

A fierce-faced man was glaring at them across the gate

sun. "I think he's lost a skewbald horse, too!"

The Police Tent at the County Show had been intended as a public service, help for lost children and a headquarters for the Police Car Driving Demonstration—not a cross between a Red Indian pow-wow and a circus.

Four large skewbalds stood in front of the tent, towering over the three "pinto" ponies, though only Fancy Fellow still looked "real", the others having faded to roan splodges, and Lady Luck, still immaculately grey.

Mrs Farringdon-Smith was sitting on a stool fanning herself with a programme and staring, cross-eyed, at the four horses. Monica Fuller was holding her sides and rocking with laughter, as the last two "Indians" arrived, and joined the line-up of exotic-coloured horses.

"But none of them is Muldoon," she said. "Not one of them. I can't imagine . . . I didn't know there were that many skewbalds in fifty miles!"

"And I don't know which is mine," wailed Mrs Farringdon-Smith. "I didn't know I should have photographed him, or taken his hoofprints. I should have stuck to motor caravans; at least they have numbers at both ends."

Half the horse-show spectators had abandoned the thrilling tension of a Hack Class to come and watch the Wild West Circus outside the "sheriff's" tent, giving applause and misguided advice, until they were scattered by the arrival of an avenging figure on a bony chestnut, tearing across the grass, elbows and knees flapping, hair flying in the wind.

"I want my horse," he cried.

"It—it was all an awful m-mistake," stammered Martin, stepping forward bravely. "I'm frightfully sorry, sir, but . . ."

"My horses! My beauties! My lost ones!" cried a voice, as a man wearing a midnight-blue jacket with CIRCUS embroidered on it, in gold, came rushing through the crowd. "But who are these? Where

"My horses! My beauties! My lost ones!"

do they come from? A perfect match! Can one be for sale, to replace my tragically dead Pluto!"

"For sale?" echoed the gypsy, stepping forward, a gleam in his eye, pushing Martin out of the way. "If you're looking for a top-class horse, mister . . . You don't often see a horse like mine," he added, inaccurately.

A stir was caused by a new arrival, which drew a cheer and a round of applause from the spectators.

Across the field, at full gallop, came a gypsy caravan, swaying and lurching, driven by a boy of fifteen, feet braced on the footboard, trying to hold the racing skewbald horse.

"Adrian!" shrieked Mrs Farringdon-Smith shrilly.

"Mum! I've found him," cried the boy, coming to a dramatic halt as the skewbald saw the crowd in front of him at the last moment. He flung up his head and sat down on his hocks, snapping a shaft and nearly overturning the caravan.

"Muldoon!" cried Monica Fuller. "It's Muldoon!"

Doctor's Orders

by JENNIFER WHARTON

Now that Roustabout had been sold, Frances Roper felt that life was hardly worth living. Everything, she reflected bitterly, was Doctor Philips' fault. It was he who had said that she could not ride again and must go swimming instead. She had always liked swimming before, but now she hated it because she had been made to use it as a substitute for riding, and to her it was a very poor substitute.

Frances looked down at her legs with contempt and remembered that fateful day in November, so many months ago. It had been her own stupid fault anyway; if only she had been a better rider she wouldn't have fallen off, would she? She forgot that the District Commissioner had told her parents that nobody could hope to stay on a horse which had turned a complete somersault, she forgot that the entire Pony Club Hunter Trial had been postponed because of her terrible fall and that she had almost died on the way to hospital.

Frances blamed her own incompetence for her fall; the D.C. blamed bad luck and the slippery take-off; her parents blamed Roustabout and sold him.

Doctor Philips disliked horses because of a fall he'd had when he was a boy, and he couldn't understand that Frances didn't want to

Frances was going regularly to groom him

get better if she was not to be able to ride at the end of her struggle. He described her as a dramatic child, who would soon forget all about her passionate love of horses.

Frances was now attending the disabled children's class at the local swimming baths. She had protested wildly at first at being classed as disabled, but when she found out that Roustabout had been sold she would not have minded if she had been classed as crippled. In fact, she thought she would rather be crippled and know that she was physically unable to ride, instead of feeling that she could ride but wasn't allowed to do so.

The change in Frances started during the second week in August, decided her parents—yes, that was right, just after Aunt Flo's birthday. She was suddenly brighter and more cheerful, she looked as though she had miraculously come back to her old self. During the previous few weeks, Frances's parents had been very worried about her. She had once been gay and lively but, since her accident, or rather since the selling of Roustabout, she had just moped around the house and would scarcely eat anything. They had even been at the point of disobeying Doctor's orders and allowing her to ride again.

Frances did not know of her parents' concern or of their decision to let her ride again if she did not begin to want to get better. If she had, she might have gone to them and told them the reason for her sudden improvement. All she knew was that during one of her afternoon walks she had found Shadow.

Shadow was a dark brown gelding, standing about fifteen hands high, and he was about eight years old. Frances could only guess at his height and age. She had called him Shadow because he followed her around just as though he was her shadow. Within a few weeks, Frances was going regularly to groom him and to talk to him. She had managed to smuggle Roustabout's halter and grooming kit out of the stable without her parents noticing.

On a warm night at the beginning of October, Frances lay awake for a long time planning. Of course, if he were unbroken it could be rather a nasty experience, but there again, if she did damage her legs beyond repair, at least she would be able to give up any hope of riding again and she would just have to learn to accept it. As it was, she was sure that the Doctor was wrong and that riding would help rather than harm her legs. It was going to be a case of kill or cure she told herself firmly, but she felt far from confident next morning as she went into Shadow's field.

Frances had shut her eyes tightly as soon as she saw the ground coming up to meet her. She opened them a few moments later and looked at the rope in her hand; she followed the rope along and saw Shadow grazing at the other end. Well, at least he hadn't gone charging round the field with a halter rope flying loose between his legs. Thinking of legs, Frances looked down at her own. What if Something Awful had happened to them? How would she get home and what would she say to her parents? Once again she blamed herself for her fall. Probably everybody in the Pony Club had ponies who shied daily at blackbirds and yet she was the only one who ever fell off. Once again she was exaggerating, and once again she forgot that many of her friends fell off for just such reasons. Well, she told herself crossly, she had better see how right the Doctor was. He had said that riding would not do her legs any good—he had not mentioned falling off a horse which she was trotting bareback round a field in just a halter! She tried standing up and, though she wobbled and had to clutch Shadow's mane, she didn't fall over—the Doctor was wrong and she was right! Tomorrow, she decided, she would bring a saddle and bridle.

"Do you mean to tell me that you have been riding this animal for almost two months?" exclaimed her father.

"Yes, Daddy, I'm afraid I have," answered Frances steadily. "I had to prove to myself that I could ride again. I couldn't go on doubting the Doctor's word and not *do* anything to prove him wrong."

Her father sat down suddenly as though *his* legs were weak. "I must speak to your mother," he said. "But first I think that you had better explain."

Frances did so with difficulty, for how could she explain to a nonhorsy parent that she would rather be dead than not be allowed to ride, when she just knew that she was capable of riding almost as well as she did before her accident?

At the end of her explanation, Frances's father sat stupefied on the chair. What a courageous daughter he had! How could she have done all that without them guessing a single thing?

Frances watched her father's face with mixed emotions. Now, what would happen? Surely, when they saw how much better she was, they would ask Mr Greene (Shadow's owner) if she could go on exercising Shadow for him? She now knew that Mr Greene had acquired the horse as payment for a debt; he had accepted him, thinking that perhaps his daughter would take up riding, but she wasn't interested. So Shadow was just turned out to grass. Frances knew that she could ride Shadow as well as she had ever ridden Roustabout—but would her parents ever understand how much riding meant to her?

"Well, Frances, your mother and I have spoken to Mr Greene and we have all agreed that you cannot go on riding his horse."

Frances almost burst out crying. How could they be so mean? For the last eighteen hours since her parents had found out about Shadow and gone to see Mr Greene, Frances had hoped desperately that they would not stop her from riding—now her hopes had been dashed to the ground.

"It's not only wrong to ride other people's horses without permission, but it is now getting too cold for you to go for your afternoon walks."

Now they were going to stop her from even seeing Shadow. Dumb with misery, Frances let her father's words flow over her.

"It cannot be good for you to walk so far, ride, and then walk back, so your mother and I made arrangements with Mr Greene to have Shadow moved into Roustabout's old box."

Frances decided that she was going mad; first her father had implied that she could not see Shadow again; now he was calmly telling her that he was in Roustabout's old stable! She ran to the window and, sure enough, there was Shadow's intelligent brown head in place of Roustabout's chestnut one. She had once thought that no pony was as nice as Roustabout, but after meeting Shadow she was not so sure. She turned back from the window, smiled a wet smile at her parents, choked, "Oh, thank you, thank you," and shot out of the door.

"Oh dear," thought her father, "I hope we've done right."

As he watched Frances flying down the garden path, he was suddenly sure that they had done right.

They watched as Frances buried her head in Shadow's mane. To his amazement, Frances's father saw his wife wipe a tear from her eye; then he suddenly found that he had to blow his nose rather violently.

"Got a cold coming on, got a cold coming on," he muttered rather unconvincingly.

Chop and Change

by JOSEPHINE PULLEIN-THOMPSON

Except for Merlin, a fourteen-year-old fleabitten grey, and Bodkin, who was round and bay and twelve hands high and also elderly, though she'd forgotten her exact age, the occupants of the long stable were strangers to each other and new to pony club camp. As they stood in unaccustomed stalls they gazed with doubtful eyes on the swinging bales which separated them. The heavy balls of wood on the ends of their head-collar ropes rattled against the manger rings as they moved about, summing up each other in quick glances and turning as far as their ropes would permit to observe the scene in the yard behind them.

Yard One consisted of six loose boxes inhabited by the instructors' horses, a barn holding hay and straw, the long stable and, opposite it, an equally long building converted to a temporary tack-room.

"I know from experience that this is a very convenient stable," Bodkin opened a conversation with the liver chestnut mare and the black gelding who stood one on either side of her. "If you happen to have a small child it's nice to be handy for the water tap and the hay barn."

Copper was viciously kicking the wall of her stable

Pilot, the black gelding, replied that his girl, Annabel, was thirteen. Copper remained morosely silent.

"Good hay, this year," commented Merlin champing greedily, "a nice flavour of clover." He had a well-bred golden chestnut called Stardust on one side of him and a strapping young brown who'd introduced himself as Edmonton's Wonder Hero on the other. Merlin wondered whether to tell him that it was considered bad form to use show names at camp but decided against it; he'd learn.

"I'm glad they give us old hay," said the young horse, "I tried some new a couple of weeks ago and it brought on a terrible attack of colic. Two vets in attendance and Susan, that's my girl, beside herself with worry."

"I've got a stomach like an ostrich, eat anything," Pilot told them, "but from the way Annabel fusses you'd think I had double broken wind and a twisted gut."

"I wish Hugh fussed," said Stardust sadly. "He always remembers to feed me but, as you can see, I never get a really good bodybrush. I ought to shine like burnished gold, but if he's knocked the mud off with a dandy brush he thinks I'm groomed," she sighed.

"And do you have a satisfactory child?" Bodkin asked the silent Copper.

"Beastly little warble. Just like the rest of them. Buzz, buzz round you the whole time. Can't stand children!" answered Copper laying back her ears, rolling her eyes and viciously kicking the wall of the stable.

The other ponies, rather shocked by this outburst, munched on in embarrassed silence and presently Merlin and Bodkin said good-night to everyone and lay down. The newcomers stood, dozing, resting each leg in turn and not quite daring to follow their example.

Next morning the ponies wakened early and, listening to the hum of conversation from the tents in the field below, awaited the appearance of their owners with impatience. During watering, mucking-out and feeding they naturally concentrated on their own affairs, but when the time came for grooming they had the opportunity to inspect each other's children.

Merlin's Clare was fair and pretty and calmly sensible. Pilot's Annabel was dark and pretty with a worried expression. Susan had rather a large nose and a commanding manner, but she was very tidy and efficient and they could all see that Wonder Hero was proud of her. Hugh was dark and cheerful and evidently preferred talking to grooming. Bodkin's James was small and serious but rather absentminded and she had to keep reminding him which hoofs he had picked out and placing her dirtiest areas in front of him and removing those bits which he had been dreamily brushing for the last ten minutes. Copper's child, Julia, was twelve and rather fat with curly hair and a dismal expression and the other ponies felt that she had every reason to look dismal when they saw how Copper treated her. First of all she was squashed against the side of the stable and kept there until Carol, one of the instructors, noticed and slapped and shouted ferociously to make Copper get over. Then she bit Julia's back as she bent to groom her knees and finally she stamped on Julia's foot and, grinding her shoe well in, refused to move despite the poor girl's screams and cries of pain.

James pushed, Bodkin laid back her ears and made threatening faces, Clare and Annabel shouted and slapped (Susan had finished grooming and gone to change) but it wasn't until Hugh came with a broom and walloped Copper that she would take her weight off the squashed foot. Clare and James escorted the sobbing Julia to the first aid tent and Annabel finished grooming Copper—to Pilot's delight for he was absolutely fed up with being wisped and water-brushed. Hugh sat in the manger and talked to Annabel—much to Stardust's disgust for he had forgotten to groom her ears and stomach and her socks were far from white and her tail needed bandaging.

When Annabel and Hugh had gone to change, Bodkin gave Copper a talking-to. "I know that children can be trying," she began, "and a sharp nip or a carefully aimed cow-kick are very important when you're training them. And it isn't just oneself one thinks about, there are all the larger ponies and horses they are going to

92

Hugh came with a broom and walloped Copper

pair with in a life-time of riding. But it seemed to me that you were being very unkind to your Julia this morning."

"She's not mine," snapped Copper. "She's hired me for the week, so keep your trap shut or I'll shut it for you." She kicked at the plank bale between them, but it swung back and hit her which drove her into a worse rage. Just as the other ponies began to be afraid she would do Bodkin a serious injury Susan reappeared. She shouted at Copper and called the Master of Horse who built a barricade of straw bales.

"Four of us in the top ride," said Merlin at lunchtime. "What did you think of Ben, Pilot? He's not our best instructor, she's called Vanessa, but she's too serious for camp; she's better for concentrated dressage training."

"Don't mention dressage," groaned Pilot. "That silly little nit, Annabel, actually offered to be in a lot that were practising 'T' test. *'T' test*, when we could have been jumping! I could see you lot having a fantastic time thundering over the fences and there was I fiddling round that silly little arena." He took a second drink. "That girl drives me mad," he went on, wiping his sweaty nose on his haynet. "Of *course* I know how to enter at A and halt at X. I did it worse every time, finally, I wouldn't halt at all and you should have seen my serpentines! Ever tried bending your spine the opposite way to all the curves?"

"But you did *some* jumping," said Stardust.

"Mouldy old cavalletti work. Trotting round and round, deadly!" grumbled Pilot. "I had to try to liven things up a bit, but that nit Annabel gets so het up; she was worried to death just because I took a flying leap over the whole lot."

"You put me right off," complained Hero. "I'd just got my back rounded and was trying to lengthen my stride, but I couldn't concentrate with you fooling around."

"Follow me next time," said Merlin. "After seven camps and hundreds of rallies it takes more than Pilot to upset my stride." He turned to Stardust. "What sort of a morning did you have?"

"Four for inspection," sighed Stardust. "I felt so ashamed. Ben said my coat was filthy and my mane looked as though rats had been gnawing it. It was so embarrassing especially as the rest of you were getting eights and nines."

"Hey, you don't look *that* bad," objected Hero tactfully.

"Well, I feel hideous," wailed Stardust, "a real fright. If only Hugh would take a little trouble; if only he'd just bandage my tail, but he doesn't care and I have to go round looking like a scarecrow——" She pretended to have a terrible itch on her pastern so that she could bend down and hide her unhappy face from the other ponies.

"I thought you jumped that last double brilliantly," said Merlin encouragingly.

"Thank you," answered Stardust in a faint voice. "But I do wish he'd jump me in bandages. My breeder told him to, I've got exceptionally slender legs, you see. Hugh did put them on once or twice but his are hopeless—so lumpy and badly tied."

By the third morning of camp the other ponies in the long stable were becoming a little bored by Pilot's and Stardust's constant complaints about their children.

Pilot had come in very cross from the ride. "How can a horse jump properly when that wretched girl blobs about on his back, losing stirrups and giving silly little neighs of 'Oh!'?" he demanded, upsetting his water bucket and watching with satisfaction as a puddle collected in the straw.

"Well, at least you're well-cared for," Stardust told him. "Hugh said he'd had a late night, the boys got hold of some beer, so out I went with filthy socks and yesterday's sweat marks."

"Well, Annabel never stops washing my stupid socks, she's going to give me cracked heels before she's finished," grumbled Pilot, "and if she pulls my mane any more I'm going to start behaving like Copper."

"Why don't you two swop? Children, I mean," suggested Hero. "Strikes me that Pilot would get on with Hugh and Stardust might be a lot happier with Annabel."

"It's an idea," said Pilot. "Hugh's really crazy about jumping, isn't he?"

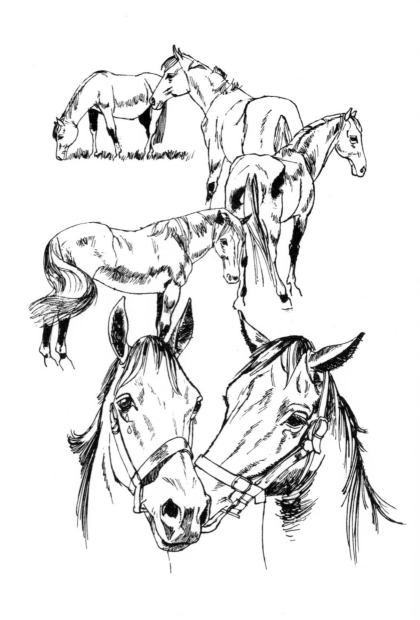

"Oh cheer up." Pilot muzzled her neck gently

"Crazy," agreed Stardust bitterly. "I shall have the largest windgalls in the pony club by the time I'm seven. I won't be fit to be seen: bolster legs, mangy coat, a straggle for a mane and a bush of a tail." Two large tears ran down her face.

"Oh cheer up." Pilot muzzled her neck gently. "Perhaps we *could* fix this swop. They might be quite glad to change us if we put the idea into their heads."

"But how?" asked Stardust with a sniff.

"We'll get them friendly then Annabel'll offer Hugh a ride. Clare let him try Merlin yesterday."

"But he likes Clare better than Annabel."

"We'll change that. Propinquity's the thing. If we stick together they'll have to become friends and when they change over we'll both go like dreams for the other's child and that'll be it. I'll be off on the show jumping circuit with Hugh and you'll have Annabel fussing over you all day.

"Tell you what, Stardust, I'll pretend I'm in love with you: deafening neighs and all that jazz. Hysterics if we're two hands apart. Can you act?"

Stardust began to flutter her eyelashes and then asked with a groan how anyone could look alluring with her mane in such a mess? But Hero cheered her by saying that it gave a fabulous wild look when she tossed it and though plaits were essential for shows, as a mane style they left him cold.

That evening, throughout the musical ride practice, Pilot gave deafening or heart-rending neighs at regular three-minute intervals. Annabel, worried and confused by his behaviour, forgot that she was supposed to turn left on coming out of the maze and snarled up the whole ride. Stardust, occupied with looking over her shoulders and fluttering her eyelashes, kept throwing the chestnut four out of step and she also caused the four bays following to lose their concentration. While the small ponies at the back began to gossip about this great new romance instead of attending. Ben, infuriated by the ragged look of the ride and the fact that all his commands and criticisms were drowned by Pilot's neighs, raged at the riders and Merlin, leading for the fifth time and proud of his position, was quite snappish to Pilot during evening stables.

On Thursday Pilot insisted that he must stand next to Stardust at inspection and follow her in the ride. During jumping they both put on a great exhibition of devotion, flying back to the line of waiting riders, pushing everyone out of the way and pressing close to each other.

Hugh, removed from the company of the other boys and from Clare, talked quite happily to Annabel, asking at intervals, "What on earth's the matter with these silly horses of ours?" But he didn't suggest changing over. Not even when Pilot tried trotting with an exaggeratedly cadenced step and his tail kinked high over his back in an imitation of an Arab stallion which, he felt sure, would tempt anyone.

So on Friday, feeling rather desperate after Annabel had washed him from head to foot in preparation for the best turned-out competition, Pilot decided to present Hugh with a challenge. He refused to jump. He slid into the wall, whipped out of the combination and stopped so suddenly at the parallels that Annabel would have been off if he hadn't raised his head in the nick of time and tipped her back into the saddle. Annabel, almost in tears, said that he'd *never* behaved like this before. A worried Ben felt his legs. Merlin gave several disapproving snorts and said the whole thing was getting beyond a joke and Hero complained that Pilot had cut up the take-off of the wall. Ben sent Annabel to jump some smaller fences and Pilot, charging round with his head too high, cleared them with flying leaps and then, neighing frantically, carted Annabel back to Stardust at full gallop and, halting with a dramatic skid, gave Hugh a challenging look and dared him to ride him.

Annabel said "Oh dear, he is being awful; it's so *unlike* him."

"Would you like to swop?" offered Hugh. "Stardust's being stupid too, but not as bad as that."

"Yes. Good idea, you try him, Hugh," called Ben.

"Done it," said Pilot triumphantly. "Now I'll show what I can do. Stick those jumps up a couple of hands; here I come."

Stardust, feeling Annabel's gentle hand pat her neck, sailed off into a fantasy of burnished gold and sparkling white socks, of green exercise bandages each with a neat rim of gamgee top and bottom, of an elegantly styled and regularly water-brushed mane.

Pilot set off towards the jumps at a bouncy canter full of indignation at the warning whack he was given by Hugh. Here, leave me alone and I'll show you what I can do, he thought, but Hugh, equally determined to be the master mind, insisted that he halted after every fence and reined back; made him jump all the small fences from a trot and then walk back soberly to the waiting line.

Merlin snorted approvingly. "That's the way to do it."

"He put you in your place," said Hero. "Made you work too; I've never seen you bascule like that before; you've been jumping flat all camp."

"Look, Stardust's going," said Pilot hastily; he needed a change of conversation in his crestfallen state. Stardust seemed confused by her change of rider, she got her stride wrong and crashed the gate. She got it wrong again in the double and ran out to avoid a second crash.

"That girl goes better with you, Pilot," Merlin observed as the ride walked in. "You could make quite a good little rider of her if you put your mind to it."

Back at the stable, watching Annabel water and feed and sponge the saddle mark off Stardust, Pilot began to wonder if he had underestimated her, but it was too late, he heard them settling that Hugh should ride him in the musical ride. He ate his feed with less appetite than usual; it was soggy, Hugh had over-damped it.

The musical ride was hot and dusty and dull without Pilot's cries of love to enliven it, but Ben seemed pleased to see him slouching round in silence and said: "Keep up the good work, Hugh." And: "You'd better ride him tomorrow."

"Serves you right," mocked Hero when evening stables were over and the ponies were on their own again. "You've got a lot more than you bargained for, old horse." Stardust asked, "You don't like Hugh, quite as much as you thought you would then?"

Pilot shook his head. "But I expect you're enjoying Annabel?"

"Her stable management is bliss," Stardust admitted, "but her jumping—I don't know. I felt so confused, you see I've learned to rely on Hugh's judgment."

"I found him rather bossy," said Pilot. "I like to settle the speed and judge the take-off myself; I don't need to be told."

"Oh but that's what I like about him, he's so certain," explained Stardust. "I'm afraid I may lose my nerve with Annabel. A few more mistakes like we made today and I'd be right off jumping. My nerve gone, a confirmed refuser in a matter of weeks." They both sighed.

"My poor knees," Stardust went on. "I gave them a terrible rap on the gate and I'm sure they're swelling."

"Jumping's no fun if someone's bossing you the whole time," grumbled Pilot.

All the ponies lay down early that night. Camp was proving exhausting, even Copper seemed subdued and Bodkin, who'd taken James round the cross-country, said she was absolutely cooked.

Merlin slept deeply until about two a.m. when he was wakened abruptly by an unfamiliar sound. He scrambled to his feet and turned to look across the yard. Then he snorted to wake the others. "Bodkin," he said quietly, "take a look at the tackroom. Some strangers have just driven up in that van and, unless my eyes deceive me, they're putting saddles into it."

"Saddles? Our saddles?" asked Hero scrabbling to his feet. "Oh, no. Not my new spring tree jumping saddle, it cost sixty pounds. must do something, stop them, neigh for help."

"Your eyes don't deceive you, Merlin," said Bodkin quietly. "What wicked thieves, but I suppose sixty saddles would be worth a great deal of money."

"Good riddance to them," muttered Copper.

"Bodkin, you rouse the tents, I'll delay the thieves," ordered Merlin and, bowing his head, he pressed the top of his headcollar against the edge of the manger and whipped it neatly over each ear in turn. Bodkin hastily removed her headcollar and the two of them

100

"They're putting saddles into it"

stole quietly from the stable.

"We *must* help," said Hero leaping about ineffectually. Pilot was trying to slip his headcollar, but he hadn't the knack, so he threw himself back on the full length of his rope and pulled with all his strength. There was a sharp ping and the staple which fastened his ring came away and the wooden ball cracked hard against his off knee. He crept after Merlin, the wooden ball thumping along the ground between his forelegs. Stardust tried the same technique, but she was luckier, her quick release knot pulled through her block of wood and she was free with only a dangling rope.

"Are we going to help Merlin?" she asked.

"Play it by ear," said Pilot, trying to make up his mind. "Bodkin's done her stuff, I can hear the humans coming."

Bodkin had begun by putting her head into the staff tents and sneezing loudly. The senior boys were firmly laced in so she'd risked a neigh and then given another outside the senior girls before galloping back up the grass track towards yard one. She waited at the top of the track to make sure she was followed.

"Loose horse!" shouted the sleepy campers, pouring out of their tents.

The thieves, hearing the approaching voices and already having the pick of the saddles in the van, decided that it was time to go and they started the engine as Bodkin led her crowd of campers in through the lower entrance of the yard. Merlin was guarding the upper archway, a ghostly grey figure in the grey light of dawn. He reared threateningly as the van approached, but the thieves were desperate and drove straight at him. As he lept out of the path of the van he lashed out with both hind legs; there was a scrunch of metal, a crack and a tinkling of falling glass. Merlin stood on three legs, blood pouring from the fourth as the van swerved into the drive.

All the humans were shouting and most of the horses were neighing. Someone took the number of the van, someone ran to dial 999. But Stardust and Pilot had found their owners in the milling throng and it had not needed much more than their appearance to persuade Hugh and Annabel to vault on and, wheeling round, the two ponies hurtled down the drive in pursuit.

Pilot was very pleased to have Annabel controlling his tiresome block of wood. Light as a feather, he thought, as he thundered along, half on the grass verge, half on the drive, and she trusts me, she lets me take charge.

Stardust felt happy too. Hugh knows what to do, she thought, and he keeps me so well balanced; I'd never have dared go at this wild pace with Annabel, but he gives me courage.

Since Merlin's assault the van had only one operative headlamp and a buckled wing pressing against a tyre made a curious scraping noise and seemed to reduce speed, enabling the ponies to keep it in view all the way down the long drive. When they reached the road they were close enough to see that it turned left, but then it vanished.

"Up the hill," shouted Hugh urging Stardust on and Pilot followed glorying in the crash and clatter and wicked exhilaration of galloping on roads (he'd never been allowed to do it in his life before). But there were no red rear lights ahead and when presently the riders decided to pull up and listen, there was no scraping sound from the damaged van.

"They must have turned down some lane or drive to throw us off the scent," said Hugh. "They've probably doubled back and are miles away by now."

"They might be lurking somewhere trying to straighten out the dent or whatever it was that made that peculiar noise," suggested Annabel.

"We've lost them anyhow," said Hugh despondently.

"And all the saddles," added Annabel.

They turned back, walking slowly down the hill. Pilot felt peeved. He'd been enjoying the chase and with the sky growing light and the birds singing and the cocks crowing it seemed stupid to give up so easily. He was dawdling and sulking when suddenly down below them they heard the siren of a police car. It gave three double wails and then there was a crash and shouts. Ponies and riders shot forward, slipping and slithering down the hill. In a moment they

They wound downhill and saw running figures ahead

saw the van; it looked as though it had been turning out of a lane and had been rammed by the police car. Words crackled from a radio. Hugh questioned the policeman who stood beside the damaged vehicles, Pilot looked into the van. "Got the saddles, anyway," he told Stardust, "dozens of them in there."

"We'll go and help the others then," said Hugh. "We know the country." He urged Stardust on, cantering on the grass verge of the lane. Pilot flung himself back into the chase with enthusiasm; passing Stardust he hurtled along the lane until Annabel caught sight of the two gasping policemen running doggedly and began to slow him down. As they came alongside the men one of them gasped, "Here, lend me that horse. I can ride." Pilot gave him a horrified look. The man was at least eighteen hands high, he thought, and up to weight. But Annabel slid off at once and handed him over. Pilot felt his back sag as the man vaulted on. Hugh was pulling Annabel up behind him so Stardust's back was sagging too. They think we're made of iron, thought Pilot indignantly.

They moved on again, the policeman swayed ominously. No zooming round corners if we want those saddles back, thought Pilot and he settled into a slow lollopy canter. The lane had become a woodland track and the soft beech leaves were easy on the ears and legs after the road. They wound downhill and uphill and then they saw running figures ahead. The running figures saw them too. They parted and one man plunged down into a disused quarry, the other ran through the trees making for a thick cover of yews and rhododendrons. The ponies closed in on him. He's going to finish off his wind, thought Pilot listening to the man's gasping breath, still he shouldn't have taken our saddles. Then the man stumbled and fell and Pilot stopped so quickly that the policeman half fell, half slid off but he grabbed his prisoner. Pilot eased his back and thought "hobbles" as the handcuffs went on.

"What do we do now?" asked Hugh. "Go down after the other one?"

"Not till we've got some more help," answered the policeman and blew his whistle. "There should be a couple of car-loads somewhere around by now." They began to walk back through the wood leading the ponies and the prisoner. Then they heard sirens in the lane and moments later six huge policemen came running up the track.

Pilot shuddered. I hope none of *them* want to borrow me, he thought cowering behind Annabel. But they seemed certain that they could catch the man without help.

"You've done your bit," they told Hugh and Annabel, "better get back to camp now; you're not exactly dressed for day."

Pilot hadn't noticed what they were wearing before but now his attention was drawn to it he saw that they were both in pyjamas and gum boots. Like turning up at a show in a stable rug, he thought and yawned as they turned homewards.

They slept late. The Instructors' horses had been turned out of their looseboxes so that the wounded Merlin and the leg weary Pilot and Stardust could be certain of a really comfortable lie down.

It was the rides coming in from schooling that woke Pilot. He got up groaning over his swelled knee, his aching legs and back and called to ask Stardust how she was.

"Four bolsters!" she answered proudly. Then Merlin's head appeared over his door, "I'm dead lame still," he said rather sadly, "but look at this, here's Bodkin wearing half a hedge in her mane."

Bodkin, whose mane had been plaited up with flowers and leaves, approached self-consciously. "Isn't this ridiculous," she said, "the children insisted on it, they say I'm a heroine because I roused the tents. Of course it was nothing to what all of you did, but they didn't want to disturb you." Hero joined them looking less serious than usual and started to munch one of Bodkin's leaves. "We've no saddles," he said, "they've got to stay at the police station; the ride was a riot!"

Then Hugh and Annabel approached carrying buckets of delicious food and a poultice for Pilot's knee and Pilot, blowing down Annabel's neck as she bandaged on the poultice, thought, really I rather dote on this girl, she's *so* sympathetic. And then he listened to Clare in the next stable telling Merlin that he was to be a trumpeter's horse in the musical ride, so that he would only have to lead the way in and then stand and look beautiful and imposing and he was to have a scarlet saddle cloth and other trappings. Then he listened to Carol in the stable on the other side of him. She was telling Hugh that Stardust must have her legs hosed and then she must be ridden in bandages and after lunch she would show him how to put them on. And then he listened to the people hurrying about the yard and they were all saying that if the police kept the saddles and they had to do the musical ride without them *it* would be a riot.

Nicky Would Not Move

by ALICIA MOORE

Ann stood at the gate watching the ponies in the field—two big bays and a little grey. Ann liked the little one best. Only about 13·2 h.h., she estimated—just the right size for her. A very handsome pony too. Here he came now, leaving his comrades, to inspect the girl who stood at the gate of his field.

At first he had just raised his head and given Ann an inquisitive look, but she had called and whistled to him and now he was actually coming towards her.

"What a lovely pony he is," Ann thought longingly, as he walked with long low strides, pricking his ears forward and eyeing her with curiosity. "Come on," she encouraged, as the pony hesitated just before the gate.

She stretched out her hand and stroked his soft grey coat as he moved forward to muzzle her pocket.

"I'm sorry, I've nothing for you," Ann told him regretfully.

She had time to say no more, for the pony suddenly wheeled round and cantered to the other side of the field. He had heard the clatter of feed bins knocking against each other and joined his companions in a dash to the other gate to meet his owner and be

He was actually coming towards her

given his dinner.

"She's very lucky," Ann thought; envious of the girl. She wished her own pony would move like these three.

But Ann's pony would not even walk, never mind canter! She could kick him, hit him, or push him, but he simply stood and ate grass. The previous Saturday she had taken Nicky, as he was called, to the local gymkhana.

Jumping was first. The girl who owned the three ponies had entered the two bays. She had a clear round on each; but in the jump-off one of them became excited, and rushed, knocking down a few fences. However, the other remained perfectly calm and completed the course without any faults—the only pony to do so this time.

Thus Catherine Carter, as Ann discovered the girl's name to be, was placed first and fourth. Ann watched with admiration as she was presented with two rosettes, and felt even sadder than ever as she compared these ponies with her own Nicky. True, many of the competitors had not done very well in the competition. A few had even had three refusals at the first jump. Some ponies had objected strongly to jumping. Some were so keen that they raced round the course, poles thumping on to the ground in their wake. Some were just plain obstinate.

But Ann's pony would not even canter into the ring. He stood nonchalantly behind the railings with his neck bent and muzzle deep in the long, green grass. Catherine Carter had entered the grey pony which Ann liked so much in the games. It was obvious that he was an excellent gymkhana pony; he came first in every heat which he entered, doing well in the finals too.

When the games were over Ann walked across the field, intending to talk to Catherine, but she disappeared into a horse box before Ann could reach her; so Nicky was taken home and Ann spent the rest of the evening in solitude, wandering through the fields.

It was then that she discovered where Catherine's ponies were kept. She could only see them in the distance, though, so being already far from home she had to turn back at once, without going

Catherine Carter was placed first and fourth

to speak to them, in order to be back at the house in time for supper. She did not forget where the Carters' land was, however, and went to visit the ponies on the first day she was able. This was not until the next Saturday, since, as I have said, it was a long walk from Ann's house to Catherine's field.

Ann watched the ponies at their feed, feeling pleased when Catherine smiled at her, showing that she did not mind her presence. When Ann went home again and saw Nicky standing in his usual position, with head amongst the grass, she was very sad. She did not even resume her normal cheerful mood when Isabel, her friend, called on her in the afternoon.

"Why are you so gloomy, Ann?" Isabel asked. "It's such a lovely day that everyone else is happy."

"Well, *I* can't be. Every time I think of Nicky I feel so disappointed. I have been looking forward to having a pony for my birthday for ages. Grandpa told me about six months ago that he would buy me a pony. Ever since then I used up all my spare time in thinking about the rides I should have."

Ann had also decided that the pony would be called Nicky, and that he would live in the field behind her house. (She knew the farmer who owned the field and thought he would be willing to let her use it for a low rent.) She had found out the name of her nearest grain merchant and worked out what equipment would be needed from the saddler.

She did not doubt for one moment that Grandpa would buy her the long-awaited pony, since he was fairly wealthy and very generous. When the pony arrived around dinner-time on the appropriate day, Ann took one look at him and burst into tears. She knew she was being silly, but the disappointment was too much for her.

Another thing which added to her consternation was the fact that Grandpa was coming over to stay at her house for the weekend. He lived at the other side of the country, so a visit from him was always quite an occasion. In normal circumstances Ann would have looked forward to seeing him, but this time was different: she knew she ought to thank him and appear very grateful for Nicky, but she was sure she would not manage to bring herself to do so—not the latter part, anyhow.

However, worrying did no good. The week rolled on and the time soon came for Ann to go with her father in the car to meet Grandpa off the train. The old man greeted both relatives enthusiastically, but Ann gave only half-hearted returns. She was very quiet once back in the car too. That is, until she suddenly realised. . . .

"This isn't the way we came."

"No, of course it isn't," her grandfather replied. "We're going to look over a pony for you, remember."

"We are?" Ann said in astonishment. "But you sent me one on my birthday—Nicky, I call him."

"What! The pony eating grass on that silly brooch! It was just to keep you happy until I could come over and inspect this pony. Didn't you read my letter?"

Ann now recollected that she *hadn't* read his letter. She had been so overcome with disappointment when the brooch tumbled out of the package that she had not so much as glanced at the letter which accompanied it. But there was time to say no more; her father had driven into a farmyard and was pulling on the brakes.

As soon as his granddaughter was out of the car, Grandpa pulled her over to the gate of a field.

"Look!" he said. "He's yours if you want him."

"Catherine Carter's grey pony!"

"She's too big for him now."

"Oh, Grandpa!"

The Badger Brigade

by SELINA CHARLTON

My brother, Tony, and I sat in the shelter of the hedge in Quarry
Field, huddled against the wind, testing each other for Grade B out
of my battered horsemanship manual. I should explain that in our
part of North Devon there is no land between us and America high
enough to break the force of a vicious wind that comes belting in
from the Cornish coast, bringing drizzle and dampness. Even in
summer we can't count on many really sunny days and we certainly
never seem to get them when the Parworthy Hunt Branch of the
Pony Club comes to our farm for its summer rallies.

Tony is fifteen—a year older than me—but we were both working
for Grade B, which we were to take later in the summer at the Pony
Club camp. I think that it galled Tony a bit that he had failed it last
year and was still on the same grade as me. But I'm always telling
him that it's because he treats Prince more like a bicycle than a
pony and is far more interested in tractors than dressage.

Out of spite, he was picking out all the really horrible questions
to fire at me in the twenty minutes swotting-up time that our
District Commissioner, Mrs. Barnes, had allowed us before giving
us our mock test.

114

"At what age are the centre two milk teeth replaced by permanent teeth?" asked Tony.

I was groping for the answer to this impossible question when we were distracted by voices below us.

Our farm is set on a steep hill above the village of Powdeggie, and the road down to the village, with its high Devon banks on either side, passes down the length of Quarry Field. From where we were sitting near the hedge we could look down on the road without being seen and our nosiness had been hampering us badly through the revision session. We could never resist peering through the hedge to see who was going by.

"Can you manage this week, then?" the first voice was asking.

"I'll have to see which afternoon I get off from the shop before I can say for certain. How many badgers do you reckon there are in the sett, Jim?"

"Couldn't say, really, Arthur. I've only seen the old boar. But a lot of folks say there's more than one sett in Lower Field. We should have a lively old dig."

The voices faded away down the hill, but the meaning of what they had been saying hit us with full force.

"They're after our badgers," gasped Tony.

Next to Prince and Saladin, our ponies, the badgers were the animals we treasured most on the farm. We had never seen a badger dig, because Father didn't hold with them. But we knew all about them. We knew how the terriers were sent down the earth passages to nip and worry the badgers out into the open, where they could be grabbed, snarling and desperate, with badger tongs and held till someone could get a good shot at them or beat them to death with a stick, out of range of the powerful jaws.

Our village has seen a lot of badger digs in its time and custom dies hard. I suppose some folk still look on them as a harmless bit of legitimate excitement. But most farmers round us who have badgers on their land, Father especially, reckon that there are too few badgers left now and it's time they were left alone.

We all loved them at Home Farm, feeling honoured somehow that

He had been rewarded with a glimpse of the big boar's striped face

116

they still chose to breed in the tangled brambly spinney in Lower Field, where badgers have lived since time immemorial. Tony and I would watch for hours at night just to get an odd glimpse of them. And walking through Lower Field by day, past the many entrances and exits to their setts, I always felt a special thrill of pride to think that they were lying in the earth somewhere far below me.

"But did you see who it was, Tony? It was Arthur from the butcher's in Parworthy and Jim Davis from the farm next door."

"Trust Arthur to think up something like this," growled Tony through clenched teeth, remembering the times Arthur had come hunting with us and had plainly ridden more for the lust of killing than the joy of riding.

"But what's Jim doing with him?" I asked, in complete bewilderment. "I always thought he was a friend of yours. Do you remember when he helped you and Father get the combine out of the mud that time?" Then I suddenly remembered something else—that it was after this occasion that we had let Jim into our secret, and he had come watching badgers with us and been rewarded with a glimpse of the big boar's striped face, gleaming in the half-light.

"I don't understand that at all," admitted Tony. "But I suppose he's never really stopped to think what a badger dig really means. It's not a fight to the death, to him. He probably just thinks of it as a little romp between his terrier and the badger."

We both fell silent, thinking of the razor teeth that could slice a terrior to ribbons. A badger might be smallish and rather endearing because of its clowny face, but when it was cornered it didn't stop to play games.

Mrs. Barnes appeared on the skyline just then, looking a bit like an irate badger herself. We shot guiltily to our feet. There was no time now to think what to do. It might only be a mock of Grade B, but Mrs. Barnes put us through it like a parade sergeant.

I couldn't get the badgers off my mind, and the rest of the rally passed in a daze. How could we stop Jim and Arthur—and when would they strike? The questions jabbed at my brain as Saladin trotted round the marked-off school in the Home Paddock. Without thinking, I tensed my knees and wrists and gave the reverse aids of the ones I had intended. Saladin crab-walked round with his elegant Arab head poked inelegantly in the air. Then he rocketed off, cantering on the wrong leg. I couldn't have done a worse test if I'd tried.

After the rally, Mother always had the whole branch in for tea. It was very good of her, as there were twenty of us altogether and she was very houseproud. Her face never moved a muscle as twenty pairs of mud-spattered jodhpur boots crashed into the stone-flagged kitchen. Mother swore she liked having us—she said it reminded her of her parents' days, when the fifteen-foot-long kitchen table had been flanked on either side by harvest crews.

Father always sat on the settle in front of the Aga while the Pony Club consumed plates of pasties and beans and gallons of tea. He would blow into his giant tea-cup and relax a bit after milking before going round the stock and the poultry.

I slipped onto the settle beside him, determined to have a quiet word with him without the others overhearing. I needn't have worried. A tribe of hostile Indians could not have broken through the gales of pony talk coming from the table. The number of decibels produced by the Parworthy Hunt Branch was quite terrifying. Father always swore that the milk yields went down whenever we had a rally at the farm.

I expected Father to be horrified when I told him about Jim and Arthur, but he just took a few more sips of his tea. He always took everything quietly and slowly and it was nearly a minute before he spoke.

"Well, Pat, there isn't much I can do. I don't think Jim means any harm, really—it's just silliness. You can't afford bad neighbours when you're farming and I can't very well go up to Davis's and give Jim a good telling-off. It wouldn't be worth the trouble between his father and me—not just on the strength of a bit of talk you overheard. It's not illegal, you know, Pat, badger hunting, although he would be trespassing on my land."

"You mean you won't do anything, Father?" I cried, so impatient I could have screamed. "You're not really going to let them dig out our badgers under our noses?"

"Now, I never said that, did I, Pat?" replied Father slowly, and I could swear he was smiling round the rim of his cup. "Sometimes the way to deal with high spirits is to give the folk a good fright. *I* can't do anything. But it doesn't stop you and Tony teaching them a lesson. Why don't you get the help of the Pony Club to do it? You lot of varmints could scare the daylights out of anyone, I reckon."

"How do you mean, Father?" I begged, bursting with curiosity.

"Well, now," he replied, "I daresay Mrs. Barnes and your mother and I can come up with something."

The last of the youngsters had been met by their parents. The older members of the branch were in Lower Field, getting a huge bonfire ready. I think we have the nicest rallies in the country, because they don't just end when it gets dark. All the older ones stay the night in tents and we have a huge bonfire and sing songs far into the night. It makes each of our three big summer rallies a bit like a miniature camp. And it's an historic moment when you come of age and join the older ones instead of going home after tea.

While the others were collecting wood for the fire and settling the ponies in the shippon, the Badger Brigade met in Mother's best parlour to draw up a plan of action.

The Badger Brigade consisted of Father and Mother, Mrs. Barnes, Tony and myself. Mrs. Barnes had been to Home Farm many times, but she had never before stepped inside the pink-and-green parlour, with its chenille tablecloth and brocade curtains, upright piano and glass-fronted bookcases. It was a measure of Mother's outrage when I told her about the badger dig as we washed up that she had taken the unprecedented step of opening the parlour in the middle of the summer.

"The first thing," began Father, "is that we don't know when they'll strike. I reckon the only time that they can be sure we won't be around Lower Field is during evening milking. Now, we bring the cows down the lane from Lower Field about 4.30 and take them up again after tea about 7.00. I should think that would be the most likely time for them to try it."

"Arthur talked about coming on his afternoon off," said Tony. "Couldn't we find out which day that is—then we'd narrow it down to a definite day."

"I thought of that," I interrupted. "But Arthur's boss works his apprentices' time off on a rota system—so they never know which day it'll be from week to week."

"It looks as if we'll have to be ready for them on every night this week, then," said Father thoughtfully.

"But what are we going to do to stop them?" I squeaked, desperately. Father and Tony took thinks so slowly. Already I could feel the terror of the badgers crouching in their setts as they heard the clink of spades above their heads.

"Steady, now, Pat," said Mrs. Barnes, as if she were schooling an over-excited pony. "It's obvious what we must do. We must organise the members into patrols and keep watch each night. When we catch them at it we'll all charge the killers and get them red-handed."

Her excited tone and her choice of words like 'charge' and 'killers' endeared Mrs. Barnes so much to me that I forgave her for failing me in my test and for barking out during the dressage section "Keep your hands down, child! You look as if you're drying your nail-varnish!"

I could already see myself galloping bareback through Lower Field, my hair streaming in the wind, the malefactors fleeing before Saladin's flying hooves. I had temporarily forgotten that Saladin could never quite be relied on to gallop in the direction I pointed him in, was terrified of strangers, and, in any case, was far too bony in the back and withers to ride bareback.

It was dark by the time the Badger Brigade meeting ended and a timid member, rather curious about the disappearance of the District Commissioner, appeared in the doorway to say that the bonfire was ready.

By the eerie light of crackling wood the others were let into the plan. Patrol rotas were drawn up for the week, and excitement ran

"Steady now, Pat," said Mrs Barnes

so high that you'd think the conversation we'd overheard in the lane had been engineered especially for the amusement of the Parworthy Hunt Branch. Mike Green, one of our more ferocious members, who fancied himself as Batman, gave a tremendous yell and danced round the fire, waving an imaginary sabre.

Mrs. Barnes stood up and clapped her hands together. "Children, *please*! I want you to understand that officially I don't know anything about all this. It is entirely your responsibility, and I shall expect you to conduct the affair in a proper manner. It must at all times be carried out without any danger to horse or rider—otherwise I can't possibly sanction it." But her eyes gleamed as she twirled her cane.

By the end of the week—a week in which it had never stopped raining—the excitement died down considerably. Even Mike Green looked a bit subdued as he turned up for his fourth patrol.

I could never have believed that two and a half hours could go so slowly. And I could never have believed that it could be so hard to keep a pony quiet and out of sight for that time.

Six of us guarded Lower Field each evening from hiding-places as near as possible to the spinney. All the places that gave enough cover were very damp and cold. We were all thoroughly fed up by the end of Thursday's patrol, and four of the most staunch members had rung up to say that they had colds and would have to drop out. That left six of us—Mike Green, Paddy O'Shaughnessy, Polly Tremarne, Tim Skinner, Tony and myself.

On Friday night, reinforced to some extent with one of Mother's teas, we met in the rickyard and saddled up six of the scruffiest-looking ponies I've ever seen. It had been pouring with rain all day, and although we keep the ponies in Home Paddock, which is reasonably dry, they had all rolled in the mud and looked anything but romantic chargers. We scraped the worst off with curry combs and, draped unheroically in an assortment of old plastic macs, trotted dismally up the hill.

Suddenly, the idea of the Badger Brigade began to look silly. I could even believe that Tony and I had imagined the conversation we had overheard or that we'd taken it to mean a deadly plot when it was only meant as a joke. It seemed hard to believe anyone would want to dig badgers out for fun—especially in this weather.

Two hours later the whole thing seemed even more absurd. The wind was so bitter that, in spite of Mrs. Barnes' injunction to stay mounted at the ready at all times, I had slipped off Saladin and was crouched miserably behind a clump of elms that marked the edge of the spinney. My face was pressed against the damp lichen and Saladin was blowing down my neck. The minutes crawled by. I yawned and looked at my watch. Surely they wouldn't come now—it was only half an hour before Father would start bringing the cows up the lane. The hum of the milking machine, sounding almost a mile away across the fields, had stopped an hour ago, as Father had finished putting the milk through the cooler and gone into the house for his tea. The only sounds now were rooks cawing, disturbed by frets of wind from their places in the spinney, circling round to find a new branch to sit on.

I yawned again. Then, suddenly, above the wind, I heard a new sound—the unmistakable noise of spades against wet earth and the excited yap of a terrier.

"They must be there!" I thought, and my heart started to thump painfully.

I tugged with stiff fingers at the escape knot in the rope from Saladin's headcollar, wishing I had stayed mounted, and terrified in case Tony's whistle to charge sounded before I could get on. At last the knot gave. I gathered up the rope with the reins and tried to mount. Extra arms and legs seemed to have sprouted from nowhere—it took three attempts before I was on.

Tony's whistle shrieked through the wind. In my excitement I jabbed at Saladin's ribs. He threw up his head, banging me on the nose and blinding me with his mane. Then he bolted.

I wish I could say that the Charge of the Badger Brigade was carried out in magnificent style. But I'm afraid it was a shambles. I'm only grateful that Mrs. Barnes was not there to see us.

I think most of us must have upset our ponies in the excitement.

Jim was kneeling by the sett with Trixie in his arms

Whatever happened, Lower Field was full of bolting ponies. As Saladin thundered across the field towards the spinney, scattering great clods of earth that hit me in the small of the back, I saw Paddy and Pepper, his gelding, streaking off down the lane in the wrong direction. I looked ahead just in time to realise that Saladin had decided to change course and was headed straight for the hedge in the corner. We scrambled over somehow, stirrups flying, and crashed into Polly, who had just emerged from her hiding-place behind the tarpaulin-covered straw stack that stood in the corner. There was a jarring shock, an unpleasant tangle of wet, muddy ponies and flying bits of saddlery, and Polly fell off. She lay on her back, giggling helplessly, her stolid pony, Star, grazing placidly beside her.

"You go on, Pat," she shrieked through tears of laughter.

I cantered Saladin up to the gate and back through into Lower Field. I could see down the grassy slope behind the spinney a small figure that looked like Arthur running like a rabbit towards the river, pursued by Tony, Mike and Tim in real Cossack style.

The spinney was very quiet. I walked Saladin carefully along the old sheep tracks that the foxes and badgers now used as runs and rode him up the sandy bank where the badgers had their setts. My heart stood still as I took in the pile of muddy earth that showed where one of the passages had caved in. It looked strangely vulnerable, exposed to the air. Surely they hadn't had time to get at the badgers?

Then I realised that I wasn't alone. Jim was kneeling by the sett, with his terrier, Trixie, in his arms. Her muzzle was pouring with blood, and she was holding one paw at a funny angle. I jumped off Saladin and went over.

"I'm a great fool," said Jim, looking up with tears in his eyes. "I don't know what I was doing, Pat. I must have been mazed. She's only a little thing—but she went after the old badger like a lion. And just look at her."

Suddenly I was painfully embarrassed. Our vigilante tactics seemed a bit silly. It was easy to forget that Jim had come to kill our

Jim carried Trixie wrapped up in his jacket

badgers. I could only find myself thinking that he was our friend and that we had made him look a bit of a fool.

As if he read my thoughts, he stood up and said, "Pat, I'm really sorry. It was a fool thing to do—especially after you and Tony showed me the badgers and everything. I don't know what came into me. I s'pose I just wanted to try Trixie out against a real beast—something a bit more of a challenge than a rat. She's such a game little dog—but I never dreamt of her getting so hurt. I just don't know what to say to you, Pat, and that's the truth."

"Come on down to Father; he'll soon see to Trixie. There's no harm done—let's forget the whole thing. Trixie will be all right in a few days; you'll see."

We walked slowly home down the muddy lane, Jim carrying Trixie wrapped up in his jacket, me leading Saladin.

It was a while before the others came back, and by then Jim was sitting in the kitchen beside Father on the settle, drinking hot tea and talking nineteen to the dozen about badgers and their ways. Trixie was hopping round the kitchen proudly showing off her bandaged paw and looking ready to go off hunting rats at a moment's notice.

We didn't see Arthur for a while. But I gather from the others that "he sort of tripped himself up and fell into the river."

As for the badgers, there seem to be so many of them now, and the spinney is getting so riddled with holes, that Father has been overheard referring to them as 'they vermin'—a phrase he only uses normally of rats that he is about to exterminate in the grain bin.

Which just goes to show that there's not much logic in country life when all's said and done.